GORDON KORMAN

THE HYPNOTISTS

SCHOLASTIC PRESS / NEW YORK

Library of Congress Cataloging-in-Publication Data

Korman, Gordon.

The hypnotists / by Gordon Korman. — 1st ed.

p. cm. — (The hypnotists ; bk. 1)

Summary: Twelve-year-old Jackson Opus is descended from two powerful hypnotist bloodlines, but he has just begun to realize that he can control other people's actions with sometimes frightening results — especially when the head of the Sentia Institute plans to use Jackson for his own benefit.

ISBN 978-0-545-50322-8 (jacketed hardcover) 1. Hypnotism — Juvenile fiction. 2. Conspiracies — Juvenile fiction. 3. New York (N.Y.) — Juvenile fiction. 4. Paranormal fiction. [1. Hypnotism — Fiction. 2. Conspiracies — Fiction. 3. Supernatural — Fiction. 4. New York (N.Y.) — Fiction.] I. Title.
PZ7.K8369Hyp 2013

813.54 — dc23

2012040458

10 9 8 7 6 5 4 3 2 1 13 14 15 16 17

Printed in the U.S.A. 23

First edition, August 2013

The text type was set in Adobe Garamond Pro.

Book design by Nina Goffi

FOR AVIEL AND DANIEL

1

There was something evil about the Third Avenue bus. It stood there, almost taunting, as Jackson Opus came tearing along the sidewalk, dodging pedestrians, yelling, "Hey! Hey! Wait!"

He was no more than six feet away when the door folded shut, the air brakes hissed, and the long accordion-style vehicle eased out into traffic.

Jax stopped short, utterly defeated. A second later, he was rear-ended by Tommy Cicerelli, who had just enough breath left to shout a few choice words at the zit-cream ad on the back of the disappearing bus.

"We'll be late," Jax predicted. "Coach is *so* going to kill us."

"We can't be late for the championship game!" Tommy ranted. "Maybe there'll be another one soon."

Sure enough, another M33 crested the rise. The boys rushed to the stop only to watch in despair as the driver went by without so much as a glance at them out of the corner of his eye.

Tommy slammed his gym bag against the pole. "Hey, man, what about us?"

"No way another bus is going to come now," Jax mourned. "Not after two in a row."

Yet only a minute or so later, there it was — the route number in the front windshield clearly read M33. Even from down the avenue, Jax and Tommy could tell it was packed to the roof. The driver was concentrating on the horizon, without even looking at the stop where they were waiting.

"He's blowing us off!" Tommy wailed.

In desperation, Jax stepped out into the road, waving madly until he caught the driver's attention. Standing there in the lane, he had a brief flash of how he must have looked to someone on the bus — a twelve-year-old kid in the path of tons of roaring machinery. It was more vivid than a daydream. For an instant, he actually *saw* himself through the glass of the windshield, growing larger and larger as the bus bore down on him.

He held his ground. Not for a regular game; not even for the playoffs. For the championship.

With a screech of metal on metal, the huge vehicle lurched to a halt. Hefting their duffels, Jax and Tommy squeezed aboard.

"Opus, you are the *man*!" Tommy exclaimed in awe.

"I'm the man, all right. If I can't get us uptown by seven thirty, I'm the *dead* man." As Jax leaned over to swipe his MetroCard, he caught sight of the driver. The man was staring at him, his face expressionless.

"You freaked the guy out," Tommy whispered. "Even in New York, it's not every day some idiot steps out in front of a speeding bus."

Jax flushed. "Sorry, mister. We're just really late. You have to get us to Ninety-Sixth Street as soon as possible."

The door hissed shut, and the bus started north, gathering speed. It beat the yellow light at Fourteenth and sailed up the avenue. The stop-request bell rang several times, but the driver kept on going.

"Hey!" came a voice. "You missed my block!"

There was no response from the driver, who hunched over the big wheel, weaving through the evening rush, accelerating to the speed limit and far beyond. Horns sounded and tires squealed as frightened motorists swerved to get out of the way. Pedestrians ran for their lives.

Jax gawked at the driver. Was he nuts? This was an accordion bus, not a race car! City roads were crowded, with stoplights on every corner, and the guy had the pedal to the metal!

"Dude, this is the best bus in New York!" Tommy exclaimed. "We might just make it after all."

Wordlessly, Jax watched out the window as the blocks flashed by. Lights turned red, but the driver plowed straight through. Cross traffic screeched to a halt. There was a crunch as a taxi tried to reverse out of the path of the hurtling M33 and bashed in the front grille of an SUV.

The passengers' reactions morphed from surprise to anger to outright panic.

"Are you crazy, mister?"

"You caused an accident back there!"

"You're a mile and a half past my stop!"

"You'll get us all killed!"

"I'm calling the cops!"

As they barreled across Fifty-Ninth Street, a slow-moving garbage truck lumbered directly into their path. The driver yanked the wheel so abruptly that his head bumped against the side window. Passengers were tossed from their seats, and standees swayed violently, hanging on for dear life. Screams rang out and cell phones hit the floor. Jax clung to the rail to avoid being thrown down the entrance steps. Tommy was pressed against the door. The whole interior vibrated like a guitar string.

The bus shot the gap between the truck and a row of taxis, rattled over some construction plates, and rocketed on. They were now the undisputed kings of the road. Pedestrians and cars scattered to get out of their way. It took no more than a peek in the rearview mirror to convince a motorist that he or she wanted no quarrel with this speeding juggernaut plowing up the avenue, its accordion-attached back oscillating like the tail of a shark.

Inside was pandemonium — angry shouts, terrified screams, and even prayers. One man was out of his seat, trying to wrestle the wheel away from the driver, who was holding him off with a stiff arm.

Jax's wide eyes met Tommy's. At this point, basketball was the last thing on their minds. What was going on here? Exactly how scared should they be? Both were city kids, tough to impress. Yet they'd heard stories of people snapping and doing crazy things. Was that what was happening to the driver? And was it just bad luck that had put them on this bus the very day he chose to flash out in a blaze of demented glory?

The shrieking of brakes was earsplitting. Pocketbooks and loose objects were airborne. Businessmen went down like dominoes. Jax was slammed into a bulkhead. Tommy was tossed on top of him. At the last moment, Jax held up his gym bag, preventing a head-to-head collision that would have knocked both of them unconscious. In a few devastating seconds, the bus had jolted from speeding missile to a shattering, complete stop.

The door hissed open. "Ninety-Sixth Street," the driver announced pleasantly.

Cries of pain and whimpers of fear filled the long vehicle. Buried under Tommy, his heart pounding in his throat, all Jax could manage was "Huh?"

"Ninety-Sixth," the man repeated. "Have a nice day."

Jax and Tommy disembarked, and they weren't the only ones. Passengers, gasping and wheezing with relief, joined the stampede to the safety of the sidewalk. The fact that most were far from their destinations didn't bother them anymore. They had fully expected to be dead. Being alive was a definite plus for the day.

His bus completely empty, the driver moved on with a friendly wave. It prompted a chorus of angry shouts from his former riders.

Jax could hear sirens in the distance. He labored to get his breathing under control. "How weird was that?"

But Tommy was looking past him at the clock tower on the corner. "We can still make it! Let's run!"

"Cutting it a little close, don't you think?" barked Coach Knapp of the Westside Automotive Chargers when Jax and Tommy arrived in the locker room of the community center.

"Third Avenue was a mess," supplied Tommy, beginning to pull off his street clothes.

"We're heading out for the shootaround," Knapp told them. "Suit up and meet us on the floor."

Jax shrugged out of his shirt and pulled his jersey over his head. He caught a glimpse of himself in the mirror. He was blue-eyed again, on his way back to pale green. On the bus, for sure, his ever-changing eyes must have been close to violet. Stress brought out the purple hues. It was embarrassing sometimes, like a mood ring you couldn't hide. Most people never noticed the changing color. Yet they sensed something was different. Often they asked, "Did you get a haircut?" or "Have you lost weight?" or even "Didn't you used to wear glasses?" Being stared at was hard to get used to. Maybe that was why Tommy was an ideal best friend. He was color-blind, and didn't see it.

One guy who definitely saw something as the latecomers jogged out to the court was Rodney Steadman, leading scorer on the opposing team, the Sure-Shot Pest Control Sharpshooters. As a small forward, it was Jax's assignment to cover the Gotham League MVP. They hadn't even had the tip-off yet, and already Rodney was staring at him. Surely Number Double-Zero wasn't afraid of skinny Jackson Opus. Rodney was probably going to run rings around him. Coach Knapp definitely thought he would. He'd spent the entire week of practice encouraging Jax with such pep talks as, "If you can hold Steadman under thirty, we've got a chance" and "Whatever you do, don't let him see you're scared. That kind of kid smells fear like a shark smells blood in the water."

Well, if there was fear to smell, Rodney already had a whiff of it, thanks to Jax's eyes, which were probably the color of grape Tootsie Pops. All at once, Jax had a sudden flash of seeing *himself* in his basketball uniform, standing at the edge of the circle, awaiting the tip-off.

It was just like when he'd stepped into the road to flag down the bus — a brief image of himself as he must have appeared to somebody else. Of course, with the bus, it was triggered by the fact that he was terrified of being run over. But he wasn't that frightened now, was he? Okay, he was leery of being embarrassed by Rodney in the game, but surely that didn't compare to the prospect of being squashed.

Jax had been having these strange visions for several months now — too long for him to ignore as daydreams.

Was he hallucinating? Maybe, but wasn't hallucination when you saw things that *weren't* there? He was seeing *himself*, exactly where he was, doing exactly what he was doing. It was almost like his own eyes were receiving input from remote cameras looking back at him.

Jax had heard of something called an out-of-body experience. Was that what was going on here? It was still pretty weird, but according to the research he'd done on the Internet, one person in every ten had them. Most often, people reported seeing their own bodies as if they were floating above themselves, and Jax had never witnessed that. Out-of-body experiences were sometimes triggered by near-death events. Being hit by a bus, for example.

But pregame jitters? Definitely lame.

Jax scowled back at Rodney to pretend he wasn't intimidated, and said, "What are you looking at, man? You're scared — that's what you are."

The ploy backfired. Rodney didn't look away. The league MVP understood he had very little to fear from the likes of Jackson Opus.

A sharp whistle blast jarred him back to the court. The opening tip-off was airborne, the two centers leaping for the ball. The Sharpshooters controlled the tip and, sure enough, the pass went to Rodney. Jax positioned himself in front of his opponent, bouncing lightly on the soles of his feet. Strangely, though, Number Double-Zero had more of his attention on the defender than on the ball. He seemed distracted, dribbling slowly and too high, well above the waistband of his shorts.

Jax sliced in and slapped the ball away. He was so amazed at this accomplishment that he stubbed his toe on the hardwood and went down. Luckily, Tommy snatched up the ball and passed it crosscourt to Dante Marsh, the Chargers' captain, who laid it in for the game's opening score.

The Chargers were huge underdogs against the heavily favored Sharpshooters, yet the game turned into a seesaw battle, evenly matched, with several lead changes. It wasn't that Westside Automotive was playing so well, or even that the Sharpshooters were playing so badly — with one exception: Rodney Steadman. It was as if he were in slow motion, clearly distracted. He'd hit a couple of shots. But by halftime, when the league MVP was normally well into double digits, he had a mere four points, and his team was clinging to a 32–31 lead.

"What's up with Steadman?" Dante panted, gulping Gatorade. "He's playing like his feet are stuck in quicksand!"

"Yeah," point guard Gus Mayo added. "We're lucky we caught him on an off day."

"Luck's got nothing to do with it," Tommy countered. "It's my man Jax, shutting him down."

"Yeah, great job, Opus," Coach Knapp chimed in. "You're really getting into his head."

And Jax agreed. The question was: *How?* How was he neutralizing the player who had been making mincemeat out of defenses all season?

As the players got set to return for the third quarter, Tommy put his arm around Jax. "Four points! Steadman usually scores that while lacing up his sneakers. Did someone slip a four-leaf clover into your Corn Flakes or something?"

Jax was offended. "You just said I was shutting him down!"

"I've got to stick up for my man," Tommy reasoned. "But you and I both know you're not that good. He's checking you out like he's facing LeBron."

"I don't get it," Jax confessed. "He should be chewing me up and spitting me out. Instead, he's making me look good."

"He's kind of staring at you," Tommy observed. "I guess he's into ugly."

"Thanks a lot!"

"Hey, I'm down with it," Tommy added quickly. "If it keeps Steadman off the board, you could be Miss America for all I care."

The Sharpshooters' coach exhorted his star to get involved in the offense. And Rodney responded, shooting more and driving to the hoop. When he did, it seemed so natural and effortless that Jax couldn't help wondering why the leading scorer wasn't doing it on every possession. Jax couldn't stop Rodney Steadman at full speed. No one could — not in the Gotham League, anyway.

"Maybe you're not as scared as I thought," Jax said with a chagrined smile.

Rodney peered back in perplexity, as if trying to solve an especially baffling puzzle.

Whether the MVP was frightened or not, something was slowing him down. He didn't break double figures until well into the fourth quarter. By then the Chargers' confidence in their ability to compete could not have been higher. Avoiding a blowout was no longer their prime concern. Winning was a real possibility.

"Okay, you guys," Coach Knapp urged as they entered the last two minutes with a 63–62 lead. "Just play our game, and we'll leave this building champions."

But in basketball, a one-point advantage is a paper-thin cushion. Rodney scored on a ten-foot jumper to retake the lead. The Chargers responded, but Number Double-Zero struck again, upping his point total to fourteen. The Sharpshooters were ahead by one and, maybe even worse, the MVP finally seemed to be heating up.

"What're you doing, man?" Tommy hissed. "Why'd you let him score?"

"That's the way I always play," Jax panted. "It's *before* that didn't make sense!"

Coach Knapp's face was crimson. *"Somebody* do *something!"*

Sure-Shot's defense tightened, and for a moment it seemed as if the clock was going to run out as the Chargers passed the ball in a circle in search of an open look at the hoop.

"Shoooooooot!!" howled the coach.

The scream startled Gus into action. He put up a desperation shot that ricocheted off the hand in his face, wobbled in a graceless arc, kissed the backboard, and dropped through the hoop. 67–66, Chargers. Exactly five seconds remained on the clock.

With no time-outs remaining, Rodney Steadman took the inbounds pass and headed up the court, the winning score in his hands. In an instant, Jax knew there would be no pass. All season, the Sharpshooters had succeeded by putting their fate in the hands of Number Double-Zero, and that's exactly what they were doing tonight.

The clock ticked down. 4 . . . 3 . . . 2 . . .

A step past the foul line, Rodney pulled up for the shot. Left in the dust a half step behind his man, Jax knew there was only one way to stop him. He left his feet and hurled himself into the shooter just as the time went to zero. If this had been football, it would have been a textbook tackle.

This was not football. Foul.

The scorekeeper put 0.1 seconds back on the clock, and Rodney was awarded two free throws. The Chargers were devastated. It had been the only possible move, but it was doomed to failure. Not only was Rodney the league MVP, but he was also the free-throw king. The first foul shot would tie the game; the second would win it.

Number Double-Zero took his place at the stripe and prepared to crown his team champions. There was nothing Jax could do but take his place and watch the world end. Rodney cast him a glance as if to say *You gave it a good try, but it's over.*

And at that instant, of all times, the vision came. He saw himself standing in the lane next to the Sharpshooters' center.

Now? Why now? Was the prospect of losing so genuinely terrible?

He shook his head to clear it, and did the only thing left to him in this situation.

"Miss!" he mumbled under his breath. "Miss!"

The shot went up. There was a loud *clunk* as it struck the iron and bounced away.

The gasp that came from both teams sucked all the air out of the community center. This changed everything! Now the best the Sharpshooters could hope for was overtime. And Rodney still had to hit a free throw for that to happen.

"Come on! Miss!" Jax whispered again. "Miss, miss, *miss*!"

The last word came out so emphatically that everyone on the court, including Rodney, looked over at him.

He flushed and mumbled, "Sorry."

He hung his head, which was why he never saw it: Rodney Steadman, MVP, served up an air ball so far from the basket that it was barely in the arena. Final score: 67–66, in favor of the Westside Automotive Chargers, the new Gotham League champions.

Parents and friends rushed the court. The bleachers emptied. Gatorade sprayed in all directions as the victors dumped out their bottles over one another's heads. The celebration was insanity — a howling blizzard of backslaps and high fives.

Jax experienced it from two different perspectives. In one, he was right in the middle of everything at the Chargers' bench, leaping and screaming with his teammates and coaches. And then, in a flash, he saw himself at the center of the pandemonium — as if he wasn't part of it all, but was watching from half-court.

It wasn't just the vision that shocked him, but the hint of emotion that went along with it. Inside the bedlam, he was bubbling over with the pure joy of the greatest, most unlikely David-versus-Goliath victory in Gotham League history.

So how come, in his hallucination from a short distance away, he couldn't help feeling just a little bit bummed about it?

3

The Bentley was a sleek, fast, high-performance machine, but in Manhattan afternoon traffic it didn't make much difference. It was a few days after the Gotham League championship, and Ashton Opus was gridlocked at Twenty-Eighth Street. He leaned on the horn, more as a release of tension than anything else. The driver in front of him couldn't move; neither could the driver in front of *her*; and so on and so on through the gridlock. Didn't anybody understand that he had to get to his son?

Many frustrating blocks later, he pulled up in front of the medical building just as his wife, Monica, came hurrying out of the subway station.

"Have you heard anything more?" she panted, breathless from running.

"I just got here myself." Leaving the Bentley parked illegally, Jax's parents rushed into the complex. Mr. Opus wasn't concerned that the car would be ticketed or towed. A three-hundred-thousand-dollar vehicle commanded a lot of respect. It probably belonged to someone with clout in this town, and people with clout didn't pay tickets. As it happened, Jax's father had very little clout.

He just happened to be the sales manager of a Bentley dealership.

"I can't believe it!" his wife whispered as they rode the elevator to the fourteenth floor. "Why would Jax misbehave at a doctor's appointment? I don't even understand what he's supposed to have done!"

When they reached the ophthalmologist's office, they found the waiting room empty except for their son, who was in the company of a building-security agent. The practice was closed until further notice, and Dr. Palma had been escorted home.

"It wasn't my fault, Mom," Jax defended himself. "It was the doctor. He went ape on me! I didn't do anything! Honest!"

The Opuses looked to the security guard, who shrugged. "Don't ask me. By the time I got up here, everybody was running around the waiting room, the patients were bailing out, and the receptionists were sitting on the doctor."

"Is Jax in trouble?" Mrs. Opus asked anxiously.

"Nobody's pressing charges," the man replied. "But if I were you, I'd start shopping around for a new eye doctor. They just told me to wait with the kid till the parents showed up. That's you, right?"

The Opuses made short work of hustling their son out of the building and into a nearby coffee shop. Over a steaming hot chocolate, Jax tried to explain the events of the afternoon. "He was looking into my eyes with that blue light, and suddenly he just froze. I mean, for a long time. So I said I had homework, would he mind hurrying it up? I wasn't being rude — I even said please. But he went nuts, running around the room like a crazy man, knocking things over. When he came at me with these eye drops, I got scared and yelled, 'Leave me alone!' Well, that's when he totally lost it. He wouldn't let anybody near me. Every time one of his nurses came into the exam room, he tackled her. That's when they called security." He glanced up at his parents, his eyes beginning to fade from purple to royal blue. "I guess he just snapped."

Mr. Opus scratched his head. "I suppose no one could hold you responsible for someone else's nervous breakdown."

Mrs. Opus put a hand on her son's shoulder. "Honey, I'm so sorry you had to go through that."

"Why did I have to go to an eye doctor, anyway?" Jax complained. "I see just fine."

She looked embarrassed. "You know how your eyes change color. I wanted to make sure it wasn't anything that could affect your vision."

Jax looked angry. "Yeah, wait till you hear what he said about *that*. He said, 'It's not possible.' If you were going to send me to an eye doctor, you should have picked one who knows what he's talking about."

"Of course it's possible!" his mother exclaimed. "It runs in your father's family. Right, Ashton?"

Mr. Opus looked away. "Well, it doesn't exactly *run* in the family, but there are a few stories. My grandfather's cousin — he had it, I've been told."

"And his eyesight was perfectly normal, I'm sure," his wife added triumphantly.

"Oh, sure." Her husband was evasive. "His eyesight. Twenty-twenty."

"But?" Jax prompted, sensing there was something more.

"Well, what do I know?" Mr. Opus told him. "I never even met the guy. He died when I was a baby. It's just stupid family gossip, so the old ladies had something to whisper about. Now let's go home."

"Not until you tell me this so-called gossip," Jax insisted.

"It's nothing. They said he was crazy."

Jax turned pale. "Because of his eyes?"

"Of course not!" his mother exclaimed. "We're sorry we brought any of this up. Why would you think such a thing?"

"Well," Jax admitted, "I've been having some . . . problems lately. I've been . . . seeing things."

His father was alarmed. "What things?"

"Myself, mostly," Jax tried to explain. "Like I'm somebody else watching me. It only lasts for a second or two, but it's starting to freak me out a little."

His parents exchanged a worried look.

"I suppose," Mr. Opus mused at last, "at one time or another, we all kind of picture ourselves. It's not real vision, but we trick ourselves into believing it is."

Jax shook his head. "I don't think so, Dad. I was hoping it would stop, but it keeps coming back. It happened today in the doctor's office — right before Palma lost it."

"Don't worry," Mrs. Opus said. She was a chiropractor and believed there was a medical professional somewhere who could cure anything. "We'll get to the bottom of this."

4

There were framed diplomas from Harvard, Oxford, and the University of Vienna next to a signed black-and-white photograph of Sigmund Freud himself, the father of modern psychoanalysis. Dr. Gundenberg was the top child psychiatrist in New York, and the most expensive. No one batted an eye when one of his patients arrived in a Bentley. Mom might have told Jax not to worry, but the fact that the family was willing to blow this much money on a shrink for their son showed Jax that plenty of worrying was going on somewhere.

However much Dr. Gundenberg charged, Jax was sure it was a rip-off. He tried repeatedly to explain about his visions. Yet all the psychiatrist wanted to talk about were his *dreams*.

"But, Dr. Gundenberg," he protested, "there's no problem with my dreams. I dream great. It's when I'm awake that the trouble starts."

"Your dreams hold the key to your subconscious mind, young Jackson." Dr. Gundenberg didn't seem to be foreign, but he spoke with a phony accent. It was almost as if he thought he was a better psychiatrist if he sounded like Freud in addition to being the guy's number-one fan.

"Yeah, but can your subconscious mind make you see yourself from thirty feet away?" Jax persisted.

Dr. Gundenberg leaned into Jax's face, the light shining off his forehead, which extended all the way back over his bald crown down to his starched collar. "Clearly, it is physically impossible to be in a position to observe oneself from a distance."

Jax bristled. "Are you saying I'm lying?"

"There is no lying in this office. Even when you speak an untruth, deeper truths are revealed to me."

"Like what?"

The doctor rubbed his endless forehead. "If you choose to see yourself from the perspective of another, this may indicate that you are unsure of who you are." He leaned in farther. "Don't answer. Your conscious mind is not capable of observing the big picture. Now listen. . . ."

So Jax listened — and kept on listening, but Dr. Gundenberg wasn't saying anything. The psychiatrist had lapsed into silence, his huge bald head barely eight inches away, blotting out the diplomas and most of the rest of the room.

Right there in the office, where he'd gone to make his visions stop, he had another one. This was a close-up, vivid enough for him to make out his eyes — wide with outrage, and the color of amethyst crystal. It was the last straw. Four hundred bucks an hour to get hit with the problem in the middle of what was supposed to be the cure! And what did this guy have to offer? Dead air.

"It's happening!" Jax breathed. "Right now! Honest!"

The doctor made no reply, not a sound, barely a twitch. Was he even listening? Exasperated, Jax made a play for the man's attention. "I'm jumping out the window now, Doc." Still nothing. "Better still, *you* jump out the window."

Without a word, Dr. Gundenberg left his chair and began to walk away.

Jax saw red. "Hey, remember me? I'm the paying customer. I'm still here, you know. . . ."

He watched openmouthed as the psychiatrist rolled up the blinds, opened the window, and threw a leg over the sill.

The cry that burst from Jax was barely human. "What are you doing?" He sprang over, grasped the man's arm, and held on with a grip like a steel vise. In the blink of an eye, this appointment had changed from a boring and overpriced hour to nothing less than a tug-of-war with death. And death was winning!

The doctor resisted, straining ever closer to the tipping point.

"We're on the thirty-fifth floor!"

But that didn't seem to register with Dr. Gundenberg. He was determined to take a flying leap.

Jax dug his sneakers into the carpet and began to haul the psychiatrist back from the brink, pulling with all his strength at the man's shoulder, his sleeve, his cuff—anything that might keep him inside the office. In answer, Dr. Gundenberg shrugged out of his blazer, freeing himself from his patient's grasp, and began to roll his body over the sill.

It was too late. In seconds he'd be falling. Jax squeezed his eyes shut in an attempt to banish thoughts of the hurtling descent, the upward rush of the pavement below. . . .

"No!" he howled. "Stop!"

With that, Dr. Gundenberg stepped back into the office, brushing off his immaculate white shirt. He accepted his blazer from his trembling patient and sat back down in his chair as if nothing had happened.

"Are you all right?" Jax barely whispered.

"Certainly," the doctor replied. "But I see that our time is up. We'll continue this next week."

"If you haven't killed yourself by then."

The psychiatrist looked shocked. "Young Jackson, why would you even suggest a thing like that?"

Jax just stared. Could it possibly be true that the man honestly didn't remember the horrible thing he'd just tried to do? Could an event like that just slip a guy's mind?

First Dr. Palma and now this. There was only one conclusion Jax could draw. He'd always assumed that his hallucinations were his problem alone. But now people around him were doing crazy things. There had to be a connection.

Was there something about his strange visions that was making others act in a way that was even stranger?

"You're so clueless, Opus," Tommy told him at school the next day. "Everybody's a little weird around you. It's been happening since kindergarten."

The two seventh graders were navigating the halls of I.S. 222 en route to the cafeteria.

"Nobody's ever climbed out a thirty-fifth-floor window," Jax insisted. "My parents said he was using some kind of shock therapy, but I think he was serious. If I hadn't grabbed his arm, he'd be a grease spot on Park Avenue."

"Yeah, that's pretty bugging," Tommy admitted. "But people are *different* with you. It's like there are two sets of rules in the world — one for you and one for the rest of us."

"Name one time that's ever happened," Jax demanded.

"How about Steadman? The kid's an animal, averaging forty points a game all season. But when he comes up against you, he can't hit the broad side of a barn."

"Maybe I played him tough," Jax suggested. "Maybe he had an off game. Anything's possible."

"I guess." Tommy looked skeptical. "But don't you think it's strange that you're on student council?"

"Lots of people are on student council!"

"Yeah, because they ran for office! You never did, but enough kids wrote in your name that you got elected."

"They thought I could do a good job," Jax offered lamely.

"Right. Just like the debate team — which you never tried out for either. You stink at debating, man! How about the one where you said we all should be vegetarians? And if people lose their jobs in the meat industry —"

"Okay, so that wasn't my finest hour," Jax conceded.

"Remember what you said?" Tommy crowed. "Your amazing argument that crushed the other side with its sheer brilliance and logic? You said if people get laid off at the slaughterhouse, it's no biggie, because all they have to do is —"

"— buy a pack of seeds and start farming," Jax finished, along with his friend. "It was the only thing I could think of. Besides, we won the debate."

"That's my whole point!" Tommy exclaimed. "Everybody in that room was staring at you like you'd just solved all the world's problems. They always do!"

"People don't stare at me —"

"Hi, Jax."

Brown-haired, petite Jessica Crews walked up to them. While she stood equally distant from both of them, it was obvious that all her attention was focused on Jax. Tommy mouthed the word *Staring*.

Jax lowered his eyes from her gaze. "Hi, Jess. How's it going?"

"Do you want to be my bus partner on the field trip tomorrow?" she asked. As part of a unit on the Roaring Twenties, the seventh-grade social studies class was scheduled to attend a reenactment of a genuine vaudeville show.

"He's already got a bus partner," Tommy put in.

For the first time, Jessica seemed to notice him. "Oh, hey, Tommy." Back to Jax. "Well, if he gets sick or something, come and find me." She disappeared into the cafeteria.

"You see?" Tommy was triumphant. "I might as well have been a cockroach on a locker."

Jax took a deep breath. "Okay, so it happens sometimes. The question is: *Why?*"

"That's an easy one," Tommy said confidently. "It's because you were born with a giant horseshoe up your diaper. You're lucky, man."

"Yeah, right. That's why I ended up with a psychiatrist who's nuttier than I am."

"Seriously, everything goes your way. If you weren't my best friend, I'd hate your guts. Why look for reasons? Just sit back and enjoy it."

"Except that I'm seeing things, and the people around me are freaking out."

"*I'm* not freaking out, and I'm around you twenty-four-seven. I guess I'm just more stable than everybody else."

They entered the cafeteria and headed for the lunch line. At least a dozen people waved and called, "Hi, Jax." There wasn't a single "Hi, Tommy."

Tommy took a mock bow. "I'm here, too." To Jax, he said, "Maybe they're just checking you out to see what color your eyes are today. But it doesn't work on me because it's all gray."

Jax helped himself to some mashed potatoes. "And that's why you're the only one who understands why you can't start farming in a tenth-floor apartment? Because you're color-blind?"

Tommy deposited a dollop of potatoes on his tray and licked the scoop before returning it. "Nope, because I'm gifted. Pass the pepper."

5

Roaring: New York Vaudeville in the Twenties was being held in a refurbished theater on the Upper West Side. It was part variety show and part museum exhibit. Every effort was made to re-create the New York City of the 1920s, from the vintage Stutz Bearcat parked by the entrance to the bouncing ragtime piano and the five-cent ice-cream cones sold at the concession stand. The ushers, dressed in ornate uniforms, expressed bewilderment over smartphones, iPods, and even plastic bottles of water. A few devices had to be confiscated as the seventh graders vied to show the staff the most mind-blowing and/or offensive app. They seemed to forget that the employees weren't from the past any more than the students themselves were, and probably had cell phones of their own under the gold braiding and shiny epaulets of their costumes.

Eventually, everyone settled down and the show could begin. There were singers, tap dancers, and jugglers. The comedian was completely unfunny, but that might have been on purpose, to show what humor was like in the twenties. The boos and catcalls got so loud that the teachers were circulating up and down the aisles, dispensing whispered warnings. But then the hapless performer was pulled off the stage by a hooked cane, and it became clear that it was all part of the vaudeville experience.

After a short silent newsreel about the election of Calvin Coolidge, the appointment of J. Edgar Hoover as head of the FBI, and the first Macy's Thanksgiving Day Parade, the master of ceremonies introduced the Amazing Ramolo, who was "going to dazzle you with his astounding powers of the mind."

Ramolo turned out to be a hypnotist with a swinging gold pocket watch that gleamed in the footlights. When he asked for volunteers from the audience, the raucous seventh graders became very quiet. No one believed Ramolo had any special powers. But just in case, it was better to let somebody else's mind be tampered with first.

Finally, Mrs. Baker, who taught Pre-Algebra, came forward. It took the Amazing Ramolo and his pocket watch just a few minutes to put the teacher into a deep trance. She stood there, eyes shut, awaiting instructions.

"You are attending a royal ball," the hypnotist intoned. "Your gown is pure white and glitters like diamonds. The archduke himself asks you to dance. The music has your feet already moving, and you swirl around the floor in a graceful waltz. Now dance, young lady. One, two, three; one, two, three . . ."

To everyone's astonishment, their math teacher began to waltz across the stage, arms clinging to an imaginary partner.

Tommy elbowed Jax hard enough to break his ribs. "That's messed up!" Suddenly, his hand waved in the air. "I've got to get in on this! There's no way that guy can make me dance with myself!"

"Don't do it," Jax advised. "All he wants is to turn you into a clown."

Mrs. Baker continued to circle the "dance floor," her expression blissful. Now Ramolo had more volunteers than he knew what to do with. He woke Mrs. Baker and selected six students from the group clamoring to get onstage.

Tommy let out a whoop when he was chosen. "Watch and learn, Opus. I'm going to be a star!"

Jax settled back in his seat with a sigh of resignation. There was no stopping Tommy when his mind was set on something.

Soon, Ramolo had his volunteers in trances and was demonstrating his power over them. Caytha Markakis was sweeping the stage with a nonexistent broom. Rupert Jones was reciting "Mary Had a Little Lamb" with passionate expression. Jessica Crews truly believed she was in a class where she was the only one who knew the answer to a difficult question. She wriggled in her chair, hand raised, waving madly, muttering, "Oh! Oh! Pick me!"

The audience ate it up, clapping and cheering and calling out the occasional "Don't pick 'er, teach! Make 'er wait!"

Then it was Tommy's turn. Maybe it was the boy's overeager, slightly goofy face, or how hard he'd fought to get onstage. Whatever the reason, the hypnotist decided to get a little creative with his final victim.

"Fluffy feathers cover your body, and you strut around the pen, pecking the dirt for stray seeds and small bugs. You are a chicken — a rooster, in fact — and the coop is your castle, the barnyard your domain."

With a "Cock-a-doodle-doo!" Tommy was off in a crouch, waddling across the stage, arms crooked to form flapping wings, clucking heartily. Thanks to his flexibility from basketball training, he was able to get his "beak" almost all the way to the floor as he foraged for food.

Waves of laughter swept over the crowd. Even Jax smiled a little. *Well, I warned him,* he thought.

"Look out, rooster!" taunted Ramolo. "The farmer's coming! And he has his ax!"

Tommy reacted with terror, flapping around the stage at high speed, knocking over Jessica in her chair. It got screams.

One by one, the hypnotist brought Caytha, Rupert, and Jessica out of their trances. They returned to their seats to be greeted by high fives and good-natured ribbing. Tommy, however, remained a chicken.

Jax waited for Ramolo to restore the last subject, but it didn't happen. There was too much entertainment in a scared rooster running like mad from an invisible ax-wielding farmer. The crowd was on its feet, howling encouragement and laughing uproariously.

"Faster, Cicerelli!"

"He's right behind you!"

"Naw, slow down! I want to watch him chop your head off!"

It had its amusing side. Even Jax had to admit that. But there was nothing funny about Tommy's reaction. He seemed to be in genuine fear for his life, weeping in terror. Clucking turned into sobbing.

Enraged, Jax stepped to the footlights and glared up at Ramolo. "Hey!"

The hypnotist glanced down at him.

"Listen, mister, you've gotta cut this —"

Before he could finish the sentence, he was slammed by another vision — himself at the edge of the stage, seen from a high angle. It was sudden, and so vivid that he forgot for a moment what he was saying, and why. But then, out of the corner of his eye, he caught sight of Tommy, and blurted to Ramolo, "You try the chicken routine and see how you like it!"

With a loud squawk, Ramolo went hopping across the stage in a near-perfect impersonation of Tommy. It put the crowd over the edge. The students abandoned their seats and rushed up front like the wild revelers in the first few rows of a rock concert. The teachers struggled to restrain their charges, but restraint was impossible. Total chaos reigned.

It got so loud and rowdy that Tommy snapped out of his trance and looked around, bewildered. He grinned triumphantly at Jax. "See? I told you he couldn't hypnotize me." That was when he noticed Ramolo strutting and crowing. "Whoa! Get a load of the goofy guy!"

To the seventh graders of I.S. 222, it was the best field trip in a long time. If this really was an example of 1920s vaudeville, they were all for it. Only — the Amazing Ramolo didn't seem to be stopping. As the laughs died down, to be replaced by an uncomfortable murmur, he was still waddling and clucking and flapping.

The stagehands came out with the hook, but that seemed to terrify him, and he scrambled away from them. It finally took two large men, who were not in 1920s clothing, to corner him and wrestle him, kicking and clucking, into the wings.

There was a juggler and a contortionist still to come, but no one could settle the audience down after this performance, especially since the squawking could still be heard emanating from backstage.

"Do you think it's part of the act?" Jessica asked nervously. "He isn't even out here anymore!"

"He's nuts," Rupert concluded.

"Either that, or he hypnotized himself when he hypnotized Tommy," added Caytha.

"Don't be stupid," Tommy scoffed. "He never hypnotized me."

"You did everything but lay an egg!" she shot back.

Tommy looked to Jax for backup, but got only a sad nod.

"Not true!" he wailed. "Is it?"

But Jax was preoccupied. Another vision, closely followed by another explosion of crazy behavior, like the eye doctor and the psychiatrist. Of course, there was always the possibility that Ramolo was just mimicking Tommy as part of his act. It had certainly turned his performance into a showstopper. But wasn't it time to dial back the poultry imitation?

These incidents had started off so rare that, at first, it had been easy for Jax to put them out of his mind. But now they were happening every week — practically every day. Something was very wrong.

But what?

It took a bucket of ice water to wake up the Amazing Ramolo. Shivering and sputtering, he emerged from his trance to find himself flanked by the theater's two burly security men, who were holding on to him tighter than seemed necessary.

"Welcome back," said the larger one, Joe. "Colonel Sanders called. We told him you're not interested."

"Do you remember who you are?" asked Frank, the partner.

"I'm the Amazing Ramolo," said the hypnotist, outraged. His real name was Ray Finklemeyer, but only the accountant who wrote his checks knew that.

He rushed back to his dressing room and dug out his cell phone.

What to say? How to explain it? How would he begin to describe the remarkable phenomenon he'd just experienced? With trembling fingers, he dialed the number.

"It's me," he said into the phone. "Something just happened. I've never felt the power stronger."

6

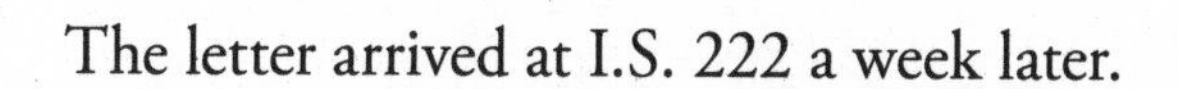

The letter arrived at I.S. 222 a week later.

THE SENTIA INSTITUTE
DR. ELIAS MAKO, FOUNDER AND DIRECTOR

Dear Principal Orenstein,

Congratulations!

We are pleased to inform you that one of your students, Jackson Opus, has been selected as a candidate for our New Horizons program. At Sentia, we look for the best and brightest among our young people. Jackson has demonstrated exceptional skills in the field of communications, and we look forward to developing his talents in a meaningful way.

Our program will not interfere with the excellent education Jackson is presently receiving at I.S. 222. We would require his attendance each weekday after school, as well as every Saturday. We are delighted to be able to offer this exceptional opportunity to Jackson. We hope to begin working with him as soon as possible.

Yours truly,

Elias Mako, MD, PhD, DD

Tommy handed the letter back, frowning. "Since when do you go looking for extra work?"

"Since never," Jax said fervently. "I didn't apply for any special program. Until this showed up at Orenstein's office, I'd never heard of the Sentia Institute."

"Sounds like a bunch of smart people who act all superior because they know more than us," Tommy commented sourly. "Like what *Sentia* means, for example."

"I googled it," Jax told him. "Sentia was the Roman goddess who gave babies their first awareness."

Tommy nodded wisely. "Those Romans had all kinds of messed-up gods. I think there was even a poop deity, but he probably never got his own institute. How did these guys find out about you?"

Jax shrugged. "I'm good at communications."

"Yeah, right. *I* barely understand you half the time, and I'm your best friend." Tommy squinted at the top of the page. " 'Elias Mako.' Who's that?"

Jax smiled. " 'Dr. Elias Mako has devoted his life to New York City education and is an inspiration to every single one of us.' "

"What are you — his press agent?"

"That's what Orenstein told my folks," Jax explained. "You should have seen them. They were practically on the ceiling. It's like the proof they've been searching for that I'm not nuts." He slammed his locker shut and slung his book bag over his shoulder. "I'd say 'See you,' but I can't guarantee anything. I'm now busy twenty-five hours a day."

"Maybe if you're late, they'll kick you out," Tommy suggested hopefully.

"I couldn't get that lucky."

The offices of the Sentia Institute were located in a seven-story brownstone on East Sixty-Fifth Street, close to Park Avenue. Winged griffins with angry faces glared down from the roof, and Doric pillars held up the overhang that covered the front entrance. The sign was small and discreet, as if the institute valued its privacy:

—— **SENTIA** ——
ELIAS MAKO, FOUNDER

The institute occupied the top three floors. Jax took the paneled elevator up to Reception on five. The place seemed less like a public building than a really luxurious home, at least one from the 1890s. There were, however, things that the 1890s never saw, like computers and flat-screen TVs.

"I'm here to see Dr. Mako," Jax announced, holding out his letter.

"Jackson Opus," the receptionist greeted warmly. "We've been expecting you. Dr. Mako isn't in the office right now, but he's so excited that you'll be working with us."

"Uh — thanks," Jax stammered. "Exactly what kind of work are we going to be doing? The letter said communications, but that could mean a lot of things."

"Jackson," came a voice behind him, "it's great to meet you."

The woman he turned to face would have been the center of attention in a crowd of a thousand people. She was tall, slim, and drop-dead, supermodel gorgeous. Not just beautiful but *perfect*, from the way her long blonde hair caressed her shoulders to the shadow of her eyelashes on her perfect cheek. Even her conservative business suit was tailored so that it hung on her without a single wrinkle.

She held out a manicured hand. "I'm Maureen Samuels, assistant director here."

As he shook it, he could smell her perfume. "Jax."

She peered deeply into his eyes and, for an instant, Jax felt the beginning of another one of his visions. Or maybe it was just the assistant director's magnetism — she really was a knockout. Whatever the reason, the sensation passed quickly.

All she said was, "You're the real deal."

"The real deal?" he repeated.

She straightened her collar, which was, like everything else about her, exactly right. "I'm sure you're anxious to get started and find out what we're all about here. Kira, can you show Jax to the testing room?"

A girl about Jax's age stepped forward, startling him. He hadn't even noticed her standing there, so overpowering was the presence of the assistant director. It was like trying to focus on a birthday candle next to the sun.

"Hi," she said. "Follow me."

Halfway down the long corridor, she turned to him

with a look that was half amused, half disgusted. “You may be the new new thing, but I see you have the same reaction to Miss Universe as the rest of the guys.”

Jax felt his cheeks burning. “What’s the new new thing?”

She shrugged. “Don’t let it go to your head. The latest is always the greatest around here. Dr. Mako may be a genius, but he honestly believes that every piece of raw talent is going to be the one.”

“The one *what*?”

“You’ll know soon enough,” she promised.

The walls of the long hallway were decorated with pictures of the many celebrities, sports heroes, and political figures who had visited Sentia. All those famous faces seemed to orbit an impressive dark-eyed man with striking brows and a strong hawklike nose.

“Is that Dr. Mako?” Jax asked.

Kira nodded. “He’s a great man. There are a lot of weird things about Sentia, but he’s no poser. He’s going to change the world.”

Jax frowned as they passed a half-open door. Inside, a lone man sat on a straight-backed chair, hugging his arms and shivering. Jax could actually hear his teeth chattering.

“Is Dr. Mako changing the world by making it colder? What’s up with that guy?”

Kira laughed. “Oh, he’s not cold. He just thinks he is.”

It was the first time Jax had seen her smile. It rearranged her whole face, made it more open, more friendly.

It didn't last long. She stepped back and closed the door, serious again. She led him around a corner and into a small windowless office. Sentia's director smiled down from the surrounding walls, his arms around the two surviving Beatles.

"Dr. Mako definitely likes having his picture taken."

She looked at him disapprovingly. "Dr. Elias Mako has devoted his life to New York City education and is an inspiration to every single one of us."

Jax blinked. Orenstein had used exactly those words to Mom and Dad. Not only did this Mako guy have plenty of fans, but they were all on the same page when it came to explaining why he was so great.

Kira rummaged in a drawer and produced a thick sheaf of papers. The stack made a percussive *whump* when she slapped it down on the desk. "These are your tests."

"The first day?"

"Psychological tests, mostly. Everybody has to do them. There's no time limit, but you don't want to drag it out forever."

Resignedly, Jax slipped into the seat, picked up his number 2 pencil, and began filling in ovals. The questions were mostly pointless:

15) I wake up in the morning . . .

- ○ a) refreshed and excited for the new day.
- ● b) still tired and wishing I had more time to sleep.
- ○ c) filled with a sense of dread that something bad might happen.
- ○ d) don't know.

87) Choose the statement that best describes your attitude toward food:

- ⬤ a) I derive pleasure from the variety of foods that make up my meals.
- ◯ b) Everything tastes the same.

Maybe this test would show if a person was crazy or depressed or something. But it certainly wasn't going to help Dr. Mako "change the world."

A deep voice in the doorway announced, "So this is the golden boy."

Jax looked over. A tall muscular teenager was sizing him up, and looking not terribly blown away.

Kira appeared behind the newcomer. "Leave him alone, Wilson. He's doing his tests, same as the rest of us."

Wilson entered the office. There was a swagger in his step, even though he was only moving a few feet. "This guy? What does *he* have to prove? He's going to save the franchise. He doesn't need tests." He peered down at the finished papers, examining them critically. "Anyone can see he's special." With a single motion, he swept the entire stack onto the floor.

Kira was disgusted. "Real mature, Wilson."

Jax leaped to his feet. "Obviously, you've got a problem with me. And that's on you, because I've never even met you, man!" He stood toe-to-toe with the bully, glaring into his face.

Suddenly, Wilson took a step back, and then another. It was a good thing, because Jax felt the beginning of another vision, this time a close-up of his own enraged face. It faded quickly and, by the time he came back to himself, Kira was between him and Wilson.

"Really, you guys?" she demanded. "You're going to have a fistfight in the middle of Sentia? Dr. Mako would be so proud."

"Just greeting the new talent," Wilson mumbled, then turned on his heel and stormed off.

"Thanks." Jax seethed. "It's great to be here!"

"Lighten up," Kira advised wearily. "He's just showing you that he was here first. There are about ten others who are going to give you the same welcome."

Jax was in no mood to listen. "I know I just arrived today. Nobody has to explain it to me."

Kira stooped to gather up the papers Wilson had knocked from the desk. It was a peace offering of sorts, and Jax got down to help her.

"Look," she went on. "High achievers are competitive people. Any newcomer is going to be seen as a threat at first."

Jax was wary. "How do you know I'm a high achiever?"

"Dr. Mako knows. He chose you."

From the wall, Elias Mako peered down, his arms around Paul and Ringo. He certainly looked like a man who recognized a high achiever when he saw one.

But a high achiever at what?

How can I be good at something if I can't even figure out what it is I'm good at? Jax wondered.

7

Every day after school, Jax took the subway up to Sentia. In that same little office, he continued to plow through pages upon pages of questionnaires. Dr. Mako might have handpicked him, but he apparently didn't think it was worth his time to stop by and say hello. Jax was beginning to wonder if the director came here at all, or if he spent the bulk of his time looking for politicians and celebrities to pose with.

In Dr. Mako's absence, Maureen Samuels was in charge. So she was the person to talk to about the institute's function, and what Jax was supposed to be doing there. But the truth was that whenever he got close to her, the scenery went a little gray. She was so traffic-stoppingly beautiful that, when she was around, everything else faded into the background, even his burning curiosity about Sentia and how he might fit in.

The clues were few and far between. There was a handful of framed news articles among the many celebrity pictures, but most of them seemed to be about Dr. Mako and his hotshot connections — Mako at the statehouse, Mako with Bill Gates, Mako addressing the European

Union, Mako at the Academy Awards. There were occasional references to the institute's "groundbreaking" research, or the "revolutionary" ideas being hatched there. Even the institute's Wikipedia entry gave only its name and address, followed by the long resume of its founder and director.

It finished with *Dr. Elias Mako has devoted his life to New York City education and is an inspiration to every single one of us.*

Right, thought Jax. *Been there, done that.*

Whatever the purpose of Sentia was, there seemed to be a standing order to keep newbies in the dark about it. Jax tried asking questions and was invariably referred to Ms. Samuels — if he got any answer at all. Half the time, the staff members pretended to be extremely busy, rushing off to be groundbreaking and revolutionary in some other part of the building.

What was going on? Jax picked up a few hints, but they didn't add up to anything concrete. Once, while searching for the men's room, he barged in on three barefoot people jumping up and down yelling, *"Oh!"* . . . *"Ow!"* . . . *"Ee!"* while a seated observer made notes on a ring-bound pad. Another time, coming back from the commissary, he opened a door to find a group of people crawling across the floor on their bellies, heads down, faces strained with fear.

"Stay low!" ordered one of them. He was shouting, as if straining to be heard in the silent room. "Incoming fire!"

Several staff members watched from a glass booth. One of them was Ms. Samuels, so most of the other details were a blur. But Jax could have sworn that the person on her left was a dead ringer for the Amazing Ramolo.

On Wednesday, Jax stumbled upon a man running on a treadmill — only he wasn't exercising. Jax could have sworn he was fleeing for his life. He was fully dressed in a suit and tie, and glancing over his shoulder in sheer panic.

Wilson DeVries was at the treadmill control. He turned on Jax, his face contorted with fury. "Get out of here!"

The sharp exclamation threw the runner off his rhythm. He pulled up short, and the fast-moving belt hurled him off, slamming him against the back wall.

The commotion brought Ms. Samuels from the office. She took stock of the situation and immediately rushed to the side of the subject, who lay on the floor, stunned.

Wilson pointed at Jax. "He barged in here and wrecked my experiment!"

"I didn't wreck anything!" Jax shot back. "You messed him up when you yelled at me! What were you doing in here, anyway? How come nobody will tell me what's going on?"

The assistant director fixed her luminous blue eyes on Jax. "It's part of Dr. Mako's plan," she soothed. "Everything will be made clear when Dr. Mako considers you ready."

Her supermodel looks had no calming effect on him this time. "Dr. Mako didn't see what I just saw! This poor guy was running for his life, like he was being chased by a pack of wolves!"

"It was a tiger!" Wilson blurted angrily.

"What?"

Samuels put her hands on Jax's shoulders. "We need you to go back to your testing. Wilson, call the nurse. Everything is under control."

It was a tiger.

The words kept echoing in Jax's ears. Was Wilson making fun of him? It wouldn't be the first time. The guy was a class A jerk to everybody, but he always saved his best stuff for Jax.

But another thought nagged at him. What if Wilson was telling the truth? Obviously, there was no tiger chasing the man on the treadmill. Yet maybe he *thought* there was. You didn't get that scared from nothing.

Hallucination — could that be the missing link between Sentia and Jax? So far, his visions had just been reflections of himself, but that didn't mean they couldn't get worse. Was this only the beginning, and eventually he'd be fleeing from nonexistent carnivores?

Exceptional skills in the area of communications, Mako's letter had said. But maybe that was just the bait. The director wouldn't attract a lot of fresh blood if he started his invitations with *Dear Fruit Loop . . .*

Could Jax be a *patient* here, not a participant? What if Sentia was some kind of experimental psych ward? Was that what made the place so all-fired groundbreaking and revolutionary? It certainly would explain why no one would reveal the institute's real purpose.

If that was true, were Mom and Dad in on it? Jax doubted it. Okay, they had sent him to see a shrink over his strange visions. But the family had abandoned that idea after Dr. Gundenberg tried to jump out the window. And while his parents peppered him with questions about his afternoons at Sentia, their tone was always interested and upbeat.

If they thought I was psycho, there'd be a lot less smiling.

"A mental patient? You?" was Tommy's reaction when Jax told him his theory the next day. "No offense, Opus, but you're not that interesting."

"It makes no sense! They leave me totally on my own in the testing room. I could paint half the institute purple with my toes before anyone noticed. That's not how you'd treat a *real* crazy person, right?"

"Well, what about the other kids?" Tommy asked. "Are they patients, too?"

Jax shrugged. "I'm pretty sure I'm the only one who's still in the dark about Sentia. I think the others know more, but I could be wrong about that. I could be wrong about all of it."

"What are they like?" Tommy probed. "Are they all as bad as that Wilson guy?"

"He's the worst, but nobody's exactly friendly," Jax replied. "They're probably warned not to talk to me, so they can't let slip something I'm not supposed to hear. Every time I walk into the lounge, I hear the conversation dying. It's like I've got leprosy."

His friend was oddly triumphant. "Just because you get picked for something doesn't mean it isn't going to stink," Tommy lectured. "This is no different than the debate team or student council. You're not crazy; you just signed up for a crummy institute."

On Thursday afternoon, a blessed event occurred at Sentia.

1409) How much importance would you attach to a career lighting smudge pots to keep frost off fruit trees?

- ◯ a) A great deal of importance.
- ◯ b) Some importance.
- ⬤ c) Very little importance.
- ◯ d) Don't know.

It was the last question. Jax's pencil was down to the nub, and so was his patience. He rushed to the office to hand in his work and find out what was next. Surely something was going to start to make sense around here.

Ms. Samuels favored him with a heart-stopping smile. "Thanks, Jax. We really appreciate all your efforts on this." She disappeared into a supply closet and came out with a fresh armload of pages. "Now you just have to complete part two, and you're on your way."

Jax said one word: "No."

She frowned. "It's required. Dr. Mako says —"

"I've been here a week already, and Dr. Mako hasn't said anything to me so far. For all I know, Dr. Mako doesn't even exist, and you Photoshopped him into all those pictures. I quit! I double quit!"

It was a little hard to turn on his heel, because he couldn't take his eyes off her. But it was worth it.

"Dr. Mako hasn't interviewed you yet," she protested as he headed for the elevator.

"That's why I quit!"

As he left the building and headed for the subway, he felt fifty pounds lighter. It bothered him a little that now he was never going to know what they were really doing at that dumb institute. But he was pretty confident that, whatever it was, he was better off without it. If he was losing his mind, he'd find out soon enough. He didn't think so, though. Quitting was the sanest thing he'd ever done.

Tonight he was planning to give his parents an earful. They'd be disappointed to find out that their only son wasn't special anymore, and probably never had been. He wasn't even sure how he was going to describe it to them — the place was either really crazy, or really stupid. The jury was still out.

Back at his building, he waved to the doorman and took the elevator up to seven, grim with purpose. Maybe Mom and Dad wouldn't entirely believe him, but they were going to have to accept his decision. Even without all the weirdness, he had better things to do with his time than fill in ovals with a number 2 pencil.

As he opened the door of apartment 7J, he was already planning counterarguments for when they tried to convince him to go back.

He could hear his mother on the phone in the kitchen. "Well, it's been a pleasure talking to you. It means a lot that you phoned personally. . . . Yes, we feel the same way. . . . Thank you so much. See you tomorrow."

Jax tossed his backpack in the corner. "Who was on the phone?"

"That was Dr. Mako."

Jax was floored. "No way!"

"I know!" she gushed, blushing like a fangirl. "What an extraordinary man!"

"Are you kidding me? The guy never even shows up at his own institute! He's probably just some actor they hire to pose for pictures. The only reason they got him to call you is because I quit today!"

She looked annoyed. "You know, I really don't understand your sense of humor. Dr. Mako couldn't say enough about the quality of the work you're doing."

"That's because he doesn't know!" Jax protested. "I've been doing nothing all week!"

"Well, everybody starts at the bottom," she reasoned. "But Sentia is expecting big things from you. Dr. Mako made a point of telling me that."

"I don't believe it," Jax said flatly.

"Well, he'll be able to tell you himself. We have a meeting with him — you, me, and your father — tomorrow at four thirty."

Jax toyed with the idea of refusing to go. But his curiosity got the best of him. He had to see with his own eyes if the man, the myth, the legend really existed.

8

Maureen Samuels made no mention of the unpleasantness that had taken place yesterday when Jax had stormed out of the institute. She seated the Opus family in a plush outer office.

"Dr. Mako is so thrilled that you took the time to come in and meet with him," she assured them. "He's just finishing up another appointment. He'll be right with you."

Jax felt some small satisfaction to note that his father was just as blown away by the assistant director as he was. Pop divas, superstar actresses, and multimillionaire socialites passed through his Bentley dealership, but Ms. Samuels was in a class by herself.

Mrs. Opus was fascinated by the many pictures that decorated the walls. "There he is with the president of Burundi. And isn't that Justin Bieber? And the Dalai Lama — with Bob Dylan! This is so exciting!"

A few minutes later, the door to the inner sanctum opened, and out stepped the great man himself. Dr. Elias Mako was taller than he looked in the pictures, and a lot more imposing. His heavy brows acted as a frame for black, piercing eyes, and his shock of dark wavy hair was accented by twin silver wings at the temples. He was escorting another well-dressed man, someone Jax found vaguely familiar.

Mrs. Opus squeezed her husband's arm. "Ashton, it's Senator Douglas!"

"Who's Senator Douglas?" Jax whispered.

His father looked annoyed. "Trey Douglas is the leading candidate in the race for the Democratic nomination for president! If you and Tommy would get your heads out of your Xboxes once in a while, you'd recognize him."

"Ah, the Opuses at last." Dr. Mako stepped forward and shook their hands, smiling with blindingly white teeth. "May I present Senator Trey Douglas, a major supporter of the Sentia Institute. Trey, Jackson Opus is my up-and-comer around here. Remember that name."

Senator Douglas pumped Jax's hand with a firm politician's grip. "You're a lucky young man to have Dr. Mako in your corner. He's devoted his life to New York City education and is an inspiration to every single one of us."

"Don't I know it," Jax managed. That song was getting very old in his ears.

The senator took his leave, and Dr. Mako ushered the Opuses into his office. The director made a point of gazing intently into Jax's eyes. Jax was aware of an unfamiliar sensation, like swallowing water down the wrong pipe — yet this wasn't in his throat, more in his head. He stared back into the near-black irises, and the feeling of invasion vanished.

"Yes, I see it, too." Dr. Mako seemed pleased.

"See what?" Jax challenged.

The director didn't answer right away. He made a great show of settling his long frame into the padded black leather chair behind his desk.

"What I'm about to tell you may be a little hard to process. So it's best that I just say it outright, without beating around the bush."

They regarded him expectantly.

"What we do here at Sentia is . . . hypnotism."

"Hypnotism?" Mrs. Opus sat forward. "You mean like getting somebody to quit smoking? Or overcome a fear of flying?"

Mako shook his head. "That is a kind of therapy a psychiatrist might use, but it's not true hypnotism. What we study at Sentia is an innate ability to penetrate and influence people's minds. I myself happen to have a certain amount of ability in this area, but nothing compared to the kind of gift your son appears to be wielding."

Jax's mouth fell open. "*Me?* I've never hypnotized anybody! I've never even tried to!"

The director smiled knowingly. "Ah, but you have — and without even realizing it. Have you ever looked into someone's eyes and suddenly experienced the phenomenon that you are actually seeing yourself from the perspective of another?"

Jax was shocked. "How could you know that?"

"What this means is that you have begun to hypnotize this person. A mesmeric link is forming between the two of you, and you are in your subject's mind, seeing what he or she sees."

Jax was speechless. He had come here with the intention of exposing the institute as a fraud. And in less than a minute, not only had the director proved him wrong, but he had also explained the unexplainable — the bizarre visions that had almost convinced Jax he was losing his marbles. The championship basketball game — had Steadman flubbed those foul shots because Jax was standing there whispering, *Miss*? How many other weird experiences could be understood that way? What had he said in Dr. Gundenberg's office? *Better still,* you *jump out the window.* Or at the vaudeville show: *You try the chicken routine and see how you like it!* At the time, he'd thought the shrink and Ramolo had gone completely crazy. But in reality, they had followed his instructions to the letter. They'd been *hypnotized*!

"The Amazing Ramolo —" he breathed. "Does he . . . work here?"

Dr. Mako smiled tolerantly. "Alas, our Ray can't bring himself to part with his little career on the stage. I don't necessarily approve, but I can't really complain. After all, he was the one who told me about you."

Mrs. Opus had been glowing all day over the prospect of this meeting. She was not glowing any longer. "So you're saying our son has . . . supernatural powers?"

"That depends how you define the word *natural*," Mako said reassuringly. "There is much about the human mind that we can't demonstrate scientifically. That doesn't make it magic, or paranormal. It's just something we haven't figured out yet. That's the research Sentia has taken on. We've already learned a great deal about how hypnotism works. We know, for example, that the use of a pendant or trinket for mesmeric purposes is a myth."

"Ramolo does it," Jax pointed out.

The director dismissed this with a wave. "Showmanship. The true delivery system is the eyes. To understand this, you have to look no farther than a mirror. Furthermore, it is untrue that only willing subjects can be hypnotized. Some can be mesmerized more easily than others, but everyone is subject to the power — even mind-benders themselves. There's no way to predict who will have the gift. But we've seen that it often runs in families —"

Mr. Opus had been quiet up until this point, but now he began to moan despairingly. "I knew it! It's my fault! It's all my fault!"

His wife and son stared at him.

"Dad?" Jax ventured nervously.

"I had no business getting married!" Ashton Opus lamented. "I should never have had a child!"

"Ashton, what are you talking about?" his wife half whispered. "You're not a mind-bender; you're a car salesman!"

"Not me!" her husband choked. "My family! The stories go back for centuries! The whole Massachusetts branch of the Opuses was burned at the stake during the Salem witch trials!"

Mako nodded. "Yes, that came up in our research.

Nasty piece of business. The temptation to use hypnotic power for personal gain can be hard to resist, especially in a frozen colony during a long New England winter. I'm sure you also know about Bertrand Opus, who mesmerized Napoleon into key military blunders at the Battle of Waterloo. And of course you've probably heard of Harriet Opus-Berman."

Jax's father swallowed hard. "Was she the one who hypnotized the Borglums into carving Teddy Roosevelt onto Mount Rushmore instead of Alexander Hamilton?"

"That was all hundreds of years ago!" Mrs. Opus tried to reason. "That has nothing to do with you now."

"My own parents!" he lamented. "It that recent enough for you? Do you know what it was like to grow up never knowing if you eat broccoli because you like it, or if your mother hypnotized you into *thinking* you like it?"

"Ashton, you love broccoli!"

"Do I? We're never going to know, are we?"

"Stop it!" Jax exclaimed. "Who cares about broccoli?"

"It's not about the broccoli," his father tried to explain. "It's about free will, and never knowing if you really have it. I used to be afraid of heights. Did I overcome that fear, or did I have help? Your grandfather ran a coffee shop. He had loyal customers. Or maybe they weren't so loyal until he made them that way." He faced his son. "Jax, I'm *so* sorry! I thought this curse would skip you because it skipped me. I guess I was wrong about that."

Dr. Mako nodded sympathetically. "I can see why you call it a curse, but it's not, you know. It's a glorious gift.

And at Sentia, we believe it will have a profound effect on the future. Your son is going to be a part of all that."

"It's a little bit scary," Mrs. Opus put in, "but it's also really exciting when you think about it."

"Will you join us, Jackson?" Dr. Mako invited. "Will you become one of my hypnos?"

"What do I do?" Jax asked. "I mean, you say I'm this big hypnotist, but I don't know how to hypnotize anybody."

"We'll teach you," the director promised. "We'll nurture and develop your gift in every way. And together we'll change the world."

Learning you had mesmeric powers was one thing. Actually using them turned out to be quite another.

Dr. Mako put Jax to work first thing Saturday morning in a room called Lab 2. The director sat him down at a small table opposite a lady he introduced as "Mrs. Park — not her real name." She was an institute volunteer, he explained, with no hypnotic powers of her own.

In Jax's opinion, she didn't need any. Mrs. Park was a bear of a woman, with a gridiron of wrinkles on her forehead and a large irregularly shaped mole directly above the bridge of her nose. It was against this formidable opponent that he began his career as a mind-bender.

"What do I do?" he asked.

"When the moment is upon you, you'll know," Dr. Mako assured him. "Remember, your eyes are the instrument."

So he stared — and Mrs. Park stared right back at him. She might not have been hypnotic, but she was plenty scary, glaring as if she was angry at him for wasting her time. He knew his focus should be her eyes, but his attention kept wandering to the mole, which bore an uncanny resemblance to the state of Texas lying on its side. Twenty minutes later, he had experienced not even the slightest hint of the visions Dr. Mako assured him were evidence of a mesmeric connection.

The director sat a short distance away, his expression impassive. If he was losing patience with his newest pupil, he gave no indication.

For the umpteenth time, Jax shifted his gaze off Texas and onto the black circles of Mrs. Park's pupils. Who was he kidding? He was no mind-bender! This was all a mistake! Just because Dr. Mako hung out with celebrities didn't mean he couldn't be wrong about a guy!

Jax had to face an indisputable fact: Whatever the reasons for his strange visions, hypnotism wasn't one of them.

At last, he could bear it no longer. He broke away from Mrs. Park and turned to the director, begging to be released.

"Perhaps it's time for a short break," Dr. Mako conceded.

Jax fled. Before he left Lab 2, he distinctly heard Mrs. Park's grating voice. "I still get paid, don't I?"

Failure. Total failure. Just when it looked like there was an explanation for all the weirdness in his life, he was right back to square one. He staggered into the bathroom. The sight of himself in the fluorescent-lit mirror was shocking. His complexion was deathly pale and glistening with sweat, and his eyes were the color of eggplant.

"I can't do this!" he exclaimed aloud, splashing water on his face.

"Oh, well I could have told you that." A stall door opened, and out stepped Wilson, his grin full of malice.

Jax was so shattered that he didn't even bother to defend himself. There was no defense. Wilson was an idiot, but he was right.

"It's not your fault," the brawny hypno went on with false generosity. "Every random dork with a set of peepers has Mako running up the flag and declaring the next big thing. First time I saw you, I knew you were a zero."

Jax had already figured out that he was a zero, but hearing it from Wilson threw him into a rage. "I'm onto you," he shot back. "You're scared to death that, when the next big thing *does* come along, you'll be out on the street! Well, maybe it's not me, but that kid will be here sooner or later. You're on borrowed time, same as I am!"

Wilson advanced a menacing step, his fists coming up. Jax stuck out his jaw in defiance. Part of him knew that he had as much chance of winning a fight against Wilson as he did of levitating. But the disaster in Lab 2 had given him the feeling that he had nothing to lose. It had made him reckless and brave. He would take a pounding in this brawl, but he was determined to put a few marks on Wilson before it was over.

And then the door opened, and Dr. Mako was standing between them. He towered over Jax, and was taller than Wilson, too. The confrontation was instantly defused.

"It isn't what it looks like," Wilson mumbled.

"Excellent," the director approved. "Because what it

looks like is very, very bad. Now, I'm sure your many talents are required somewhere."

Wilson beat a hasty retreat.

"I'm sorry," Jax told the director. "I tried with that lady in there. I really did. But it's no use."

Dr. Mako smiled thinly. "How odd that you know more after less than an hour than I do after twenty years."

"I know when someone's not hypnotized," Jax reasoned. "And she just isn't."

"This is not like chopping down a tree, where a little more muscle will give you a better, faster result. You can't force this."

Jax was growing desperate. "Tell me what to do, and I'll do it."

The director was calm. "When you hypnotized accidentally, it was completely without effort. It simply happened. You have to let this happen, too."

Jax must have seemed defeated, because Dr. Mako relented. "Take a walk. Get some air. Empty your mind."

"Mrs. Park —" Jax began.

"Will wait for you. Take fifteen minutes. We'll meet back in Lab 2."

Out on East Sixty-Fifth Street, his hands jammed in his pockets, Jax tried a few deep breaths. His lungs wouldn't fill, and his mind wouldn't empty. His every inclination was to walk away and keep on walking — to the subway, followed by home. Whatever was going on at Sentia had nothing to do with him. He had pressing issues in his life — his hallucinations, and the erratic behavior of the people around him. To obsess over this *non-thing* wasn't just crazy; it was wasting time that should be spent solving real problems.

He flopped down on a bench and tried to think of one good reason to return to Lab 2.

"Hey, kid, got any spare change?"

Jax glanced up at the man who stood before him. He was unshaven and roughly dressed in a red-and-black lumber jacket, although he didn't seem threatening. Still, Jax's instincts as a city kid told him not to engage this stranger.

He turned away. "Sorry, mister."

"Come on, well-heeled kid like you — help me out."

It was the crowning glory of a really lousy morning. Failure at Sentia, and now he was going to have to abandon his bench to avoid this panhandler. He got up to leave, his eyes locking with the man's as he rose.

It was almost instantaneous. One minute he was glaring at the person who had interrupted his solitude. The next, he was looking back at himself.

A vision! According to Dr. Mako, this was a sign of hypnotism! If only there was some way to be sure. . . .

"Your nose is itchy," Jax said tentatively.

He watched in amazement as the panhandler scrubbed madly under his nostrils.

"It's better now."

The scratching ceased.

"Sit down for a while. You're tired."

The man took a seat on the bench.

Jax felt a surge of excitement. He'd done it! He was a hypnotist! His one thought was to tell Dr. Mako. He started back to the building, and then hesitated. Amid the thrill of success, something didn't sit well. This panhandler was still in his power. Jax was a newbie at this. Who knew what signals he might be unknowingly giving off? The poor guy could step out into traffic and get himself killed!

"I'm going to count to three, and then you'll wake up, okay?" That made no sense. The panhandler wasn't even asleep. "I mean, you'll stop being hypnotized. You'll feel great. Really. And you'll remember to look after yourself, and not do anything stupid. The city can be a tough place, you know. . . ." He had a sense that he was rambling — something the other hypnos didn't do. The mesmeric commands he'd overheard from them had been simple and to the point. "Well, good luck, mister. One, two, three."

And when he was certain that his first true subject had come out of his trance and was relaxing happily on the bench, Jax raced across the street and back into Sentia.

"Dr. Mako!" His feet barely touched the floor as he made his way down the corridor, floating on air.

Kira Kendall poked her head out of the break room to see what was going on.

Jax grasped her shoulders. "I hypnotized somebody!"

She shook herself loose. "That's the general idea around here," she said with a tolerant smile.

Jax spotted the director outside Lab 2, and moved on

from Kira. "Dr. Mako! You're not going to believe it! Some homeless guy hit me up for change, and I hypnotized him! I let it happen, just like you said!"

The director nodded. "Are you ready to take this confidence into the lab?"

Jax's exhilaration faded somewhat at the thought of staring down Mrs. Park and Texas. But at this point, he was willing to follow Dr. Mako anywhere. "Let's do it!"

She was still intimidating, and the Lone Star State was a definite distraction. He ignored the mole and focused on the eyes, trying to recapture his mind-set outside on the bench. He hadn't been trying to hypnotize: quite the opposite. He'd been conceding defeat, thinking about chucking the whole thing and going home. All he'd really wanted was to be left alone — by the panhandler, by Dr. Mako, and especially by all the gobbledygook his mind was serving up these days.

And through his distracted thinking, there it was — a picture of himself in Lab 2, as seen through the eyes of Mrs. Park.

He had her. He was a mind-bender after all. Victory, as sweet as any game-winning three-point shot.

Most satisfying of all was the praise from the great man himself. "Excellent work, Jackson — although I should tell you that I'm not surprised. You have the gift, like generations of Opuses before you. Congratulations."

Jax beamed. "Thanks, Dr. Mako."

"However," the director went on, his expression solemn, "your developing talent belongs not only to you, but to all humanity. You must never use it for personal gain, to exact revenge, or to take advantage of another."

"I'd never do anything like that —"

Dr. Mako cut him off. "The temptations will be great. Even if you think your actions are harmless, you must not resort to hypnotism for frivolous or recreational purposes. This is our number-one rule at Sentia, and it applies to all of us, myself included. This is a zero-tolerance policy. Violators will be expelled from the institute, no exceptions."

"I understand." It was a sobering lecture, but nothing could have spoiled Jax's good mood. He had spent many days at the office on East Sixty-Fifth Street, yet this was the first time he felt as if he truly belonged.

He was on his way out, waiting for the elevator, when he came upon a sight that gave him even more to think about than his recent triumphs. Ms. Samuels's office door was open a crack, and he could see someone in the visitor's chair, someone counting a handful of bills.

Someone in a red-and-black lumber jacket.

Tommy thought it was all a joke. “What are you going to do? Turn me into a frog?”

“It’s not magic,” Jax explained patiently. “It’s hypnotism. It’s a totally real thing. It’s been running in my father’s family forever.”

Even though Jax believed it 100 percent, he had to admit that it sounded like baloney. Especially to Tommy, who was kind of noncreative and only trusted what he could see — in black and white — with his own eyes.

They shuffled forward in the cafeteria line. Tommy took two trays from the rack and handed one to Jax. “Just because your dad had a lot of wacko relatives doesn’t make you the sorcerer’s apprentice. Every family has a few ding-dongs. You wouldn’t believe what some of the Cicerellis were up to back in the old country.”

“There’s no way everything that’s been happening to me is a coincidence,” Jax insisted. “All the visions, the weird things people are doing around me. You said yourself how lucky I am. I don’t think I’m lucky. I think I’m bending people without even knowing I’m doing it.”

“Bending?”

"Hypnotizing," Jax supplied. "They sometimes call us mind-benders."

"Fine," Tommy all but growled. "Show me. Bend my mind."

"What, here?"

"Why not?" Tommy challenged. "You're so powerful — it should be easy."

"All right, but I'm not that good yet." He turned and peered directly into Tommy's eyes, not sure what to do beyond staring. He was still enough of a novice that if the mesmeric link didn't start on its own, he was lost. Even Dr. Mako conceded that there was no mental switch that could be flipped to start hypnotizing — at least none that Sentia had been able to identify so far.

"Ooooh!" Tommy intoned in an eerie voice. "I feel my mind bending! My mind is very crooked. What should I do, master? Eat lunch? Rob a bank? Flush myself down the nearest toilet?"

"Do you want to do this or not?" Jax demanded. He stared at his friend with an increased degree of concentration. There was no vision of himself through Tommy's gaze. At the institute, Dr. Mako had told him exactly what to look for. It was almost like a picture-in-picture image on a TV. There was no sign of it here. "It's not working," he admitted. "It might be because you're color-blind."

"I was color-blind for that Ramolo guy, too," Tommy reminded him, "and he still got me to go all poultry."

"Every hypno's eyes find a different entry into the

subject's mind," Jax lectured, quoting Dr. Mako. "Mine are all about color. Ramolo's must work in some other way."

Tommy placed a chocolate-milk container on his tray. "Well, do somebody else, then." He indicated a tall, slender brunette two places ahead of them in the line. "How about Lisa Sweeney? Can't hurt to have an eighth-grade cheerleader in your power."

Dr. Mako's lecture replayed itself in Jax's mind, especially terms like *zero tolerance* and *expelled from the institute*. But this wouldn't be for frivolous or recreational purposes. Jax had to convince his best friend that all this was real. After Mom and Dad, Tommy was the most important person in his life. They always told each other everything. Besides, it was impossible to blow off a dare from Tommy Cicerelli. He'd nag you until you saw it through.

Jax focused his attention on the tall girl's pretty profile. It was a little hard at first, since Lisa was looking at the salad bar, not at him. Slowly but surely, he worked her gaze over in his direction. He had her!

She glared at him. "Go stalk somebody else, dweeb."

Tommy laughed in his face. "You did it, man! You hypnotized her into insulting you!"

Jax was bewildered. He was feeling a connection, could even see the PIP image of himself from another point of view. But it couldn't be Lisa. . . .

All at once, Tommy squeezed his arm. "Look!"

As the cheerleader picked up her tray and moved on, they could both see the lunch lady on the other side of the salad bar, unmoving, her eyes fixed on Jax. If anyone had ever been in a hypnotic trance, it was her.

"Dude!" Tommy hissed. "You zonked out the lunch lady!"

Jax couldn't contain a goofy grin. Okay, she wasn't exactly the subject he'd been aiming for. But he'd done it! Not by accident, not in a lab situation, but right out here in the real world. Well, the cafeteria . . .

"Okay." Tommy rubbed his hands together. "What are we going to make her do?"

"Nothing. I'm not supposed to use hypnotism for frivolous purposes."

"This isn't frivolous!" Tommy insisted. "It's awesome! Make her bark like a dog!"

"Forget it, Tommy. She works here. How would you feel if she got fired because she wasn't doing her job?"

"So make her do something that's part of her job," Tommy wheedled. "She never puts enough gravy on the Salisbury steak. She holds on to the stuff like it's her own blood. Make her give me a decent amount. And on the mashed potatoes, too. That's not frivolous. That's customer satisfaction."

Jax looked his friend in the eye. "Just gravy."

"And maybe a free chocolate-chip cookie."

"No chance. You get what you paid for, and nothing more."

This was definitely not what Dr. Mako had in mind. But as long as his command never went beyond serving lunch, it should be okay. Besides, this might be the first time that an innocent bystander had been bent by a mesmeric attempt that missed its target. So this counted as real research.

When he reached the salad bar, he leaned over the sneeze guard into the lunch lady's face and murmured, "My friend here likes a lot of gravy. Make sure you give him as much as you can. When the next bell rings, you'll remember nothing of this conversation." He got his own lunch and carried it to an empty table.

The first bite had not yet reached his lips when the commotion started up from the food line.

"Okay! That's enough! I'm good! Stop! *Stop!*" A moment later, Tommy appeared, his tray dripping gravy. The lunch lady was right behind him, a ladle in one hand and the gravy pot in the other. "Opus, help! Hit the off switch!"

"Stop!" Jax said urgently. Louder: *"Stop!"*

But the woman continued to follow Tommy, spooning ladle after ladle onto his swamped tray. Jax realized with some alarm that the mesmeric link between them no longer existed. He had no PIP image through her eyes. All that remained was his command: *Give him as much as you can.* He tried to catch her eye and re-hypnotize her. But she was so focused on the need to deposit as much gravy as possible onto Tommy's plate that she wouldn't look in his direction.

Jax felt a rising panic. He had completely lost control of the situation. All around the cafeteria, kids were interrupting their lunches to watch the great gravy chase. It was only a matter of time before a teacher noticed. Then that poor lunch lady was going to be in big trouble, and all because Jax had broken Sentia's number-one rule.

The general murmur of surprise was turning into a cheer as the excess gravy poured over the side of the tray. A passing sneaker slid in the puddle, and a sixth grader went down. It got a round of applause from the cafeteria crowd, which grew to a standing ovation as his flying meal sprayed soup over a wide area. At that moment, the parade from the food line reached the slick, and the wipeouts grew more spectacular. Shoes slipped, trays tipped. Total chaos reigned.

"How about a little help here?" Tommy cried.

Jax had to stop this before it escalated into a full-scale riot. Trouble at school was bad enough, but what about Sentia? If news of this somehow got back to Dr. Mako, Jax would have a lot of difficulty explaining how this didn't count as frivolous.

With that random thought, help came from an unexpected quarter. The bell rang. The lunch lady took her ladle and her pot and quietly returned to her post. It was obvious that she had no recollection of the ruckus that had just ended.

Tommy set down his tray with a splash and looked at his entrée, floating in an ocean of brown. "Okay, I admit it. You're a hypnotist, all right. The worst hypnotist in the world, but you can definitely do it."

Jax made a face. "Be quiet and drink your lunch."

11

Most of the experiment subjects at Sentia were volunteers who were paid fifty dollars a day to participate in "brain studies." This brought in an interesting combination of college students and homeless people for the hypnos to work on. Few, if any, remembered the details of what happened to them at Sentia. Ray Finklemeyer — the Amazing Ramolo himself — was charged with implanting a post-hypnotic suggestion in the newcomers. Upon leaving the building, they were instructed to forget everything.

"Just once," Wilson grumbled, peering out the lounge window as the volunteers filed inside, "I'd like to bend somebody who isn't already *used* by the time he gets to me."

"Used?" Jax repeated.

"He means that the subjects already carry some hypnotic architecture by the time we see them," Kira explained. "But it's nothing that would affect our work with them."

"Says Ray," Wilson countered. "What's to stop the staff from adding a little spy suggestion to rat out anybody who might be getting his jollies messing with heads?"

Jax was genuinely mystified. "Who would do that?"

The burly hypno glared at him. "You don't know anything, do you? You were born, like, yesterday."

Jax's first subject that day was Mr. Baltic. Sentia volunteers never used their real names. Jax wasn't sure why, but the aliases usually came from a Monopoly board — Vermont, Pacific, Reading. Mrs. Park was short for Park Place. Jax's panhandler, the man in the lumber jacket, turned out to be a regular named Mr. St. James.

Jax gave the young man across the table a double-barreled shot of his large color-changing eyes. The result was almost instantaneous. He was looking back at himself, the image faint, but absolutely distinct. He resisted the urge to glance over at Dr. Mako, who was overseeing the exercise.

"Okay," Jax instructed the subject. "I need you to get out of your chair and jump up and down."

Mr. Baltic stood up slowly and began to hop in place in an orderly, unruffled way.

This time, Jax did risk a look over at the director. Mako's face was impassive, but surely he had to appreciate how quickly Jax had produced the required action.

At the next table, another hypno, Augie Cunningham, stood his subject up and said, "You're standing on a bed of hot coals. If you stay at rest for even a second, the soles of your feet will be badly burned." That was all it took to have Mrs. Tennessee up and dancing with great urgency.

Jax regarded Mr. Baltic's halfhearted methodical jumps. Although Mrs. Tennessee was a middle-aged woman, Augie had generated a much higher energy level.

Mako looked on approvingly.

The third and final mind-bender took her turn. It was Kira Kendall. "A group of children is trapped in a burning house," she told Mr. St. Charles in an impassioned voice. "Flames lick at them from the walls, and the room is filling up with smoke. Only you can save them! Your feet operate a pump that sprays water on the fire. Quickly! Pump! Their lives depend on you!"

The reaction was nothing short of astounding. The subject's legs hammered like pistons in his mad effort to save the nonexistent children Kira had placed in his mind.

Mako was smiling and applauding. "Well done, Kira. Masterful. What you've shown us is that it's not just a matter of whether someone is hypnotized; the important thing is what we construct in their minds while they're under. A simple instruction is not as powerful as a feeling, like fire on your skin. And even that is not as powerful as something that speaks to your moral character, like saving the lives of the innocent."

Jax shuffled out of the room the loser, the hypnotist who had performed the worst. Why was he the lousiest? What had happened to all the great potential Mako had spoken about?

The director must have noticed his crestfallen expression because, afterward, he pulled Jax aside. "Don't be discouraged, Jackson. All the things that you lack can be learned. But a natural gift can never be created if it isn't there in the first place."

Saturdays at Sentia were the marathon days, since the hypnos came early and stayed late. The workload was intense, and included far more than hands-on experiments with volunteers. Jax and the others also studied the history of hypnotism and the lives of great practitioners of the art, like the monk Rasputin, and the legendary Dr. Mesmer.

Jax was amazed to learn how often hypnotism had played a part in key world events. Sir Edmund Hillary would never have conquered Mount Everest if he hadn't been mesmerized to get over his fear of heights. Brahms was tone-deaf, and wouldn't have been able to write halfway-decent music if his wife hadn't been a gifted mind-bender. Lewis and Clark were both hypnotists, and had bent each other no less than twenty-seven times before they reached the Pacific. It was the only thing that kept them going.

The list went on and on. Some of the finest achievements, like the invention of the telephone; the most terrible disasters, like the Hindenburg tragedy; and the most daring crimes, like the Great Train Robbery, all had a hypnotic connection. Jax was startled to note how often the name Opus came up. No wonder Mako had scouted Jax for Sentia. Dad's family was in it up to their necks. Scarcely did a generation pass without an Opus in the headlines.

"Wipe that grin off your face, Dopus," Wilson snarled at Jax in the lounge during a break. "You may have a famous name, but the legend dies with you. You couldn't hypnotize your way out of a wet paper bag."

Kira rolled her eyes. "He just got here, Wilson. How many of us were as good as Mesmer in our first week?"

If Sentia had a schoolyard bully, it was definitely Wilson. But all the hypnos were standoffish. Kira had an innate sense of fairness that refused to let Wilson ride roughshod over the others. But she was too serious and dedicated to her craft to be very friendly. She was the best mind-bender because she tried ten times harder than everybody else. She was all work and no play. Not that there was much opportunity for playing at Sentia.

At seventeen, Augie was the oldest, and had been at the institute the longest. Although he had the most experience, it was plain that he had absolutely no sense of humor. He never even smiled, much less laughed, and making a joke was out of the question. Jax, who had always equated humor with intelligence, wondered if Augie would ever be able to think on his feet well enough to be a top-notch mind-bender.

There were the two Lancaster Singhs, first cousins named after a common grandfather. They were best friends, and competitive to the point of insanity. Each one thought he could be *the* Lancaster Singh by outmesmerizing the other. The result was that these two talented hypnos expended so much energy bending each other that they had very little left to devote to the institute. Wilson called them Singh One and Singh Two. The guy was a lunkhead, but never at a loss for a nickname.

Grace Cavanaugh was a nationally ranked tennis

player, and was constantly cutting short her work at the institute to rush off to a match or tournament. Natalie Ziegler was confined to a wheelchair, yet her piercing gaze enabled her to entrance a subject faster than any of them, except possibly Jax. DeRon Marcus was Wilson's sidekick. He could be perfectly normal, and even nice. But then Wilson would walk into the room and DeRon's pleasant personality would shut off.

During Jax's second week at Sentia, there was also a red-haired girl of about sixteen, but by Saturday she was nowhere to be found.

"Does anyone know what happened to Clarissa?" he asked the others. His answer was no answer, a vaguely uneasy hum in the lounge. "I hope she isn't really sick or anything like that." More humming.

It was Singh Two who finally provided an explanation. "She isn't sick."

"She *might* be sick," Singh One amended. "But the reason why she isn't here has nothing to do with her health."

Jax must have looked bewildered, because Wilson burst out, "Will somebody just tell him? She washed out, Dopus. They gave her the boot."

Jax was shocked. "But why? Did she do something wrong?"

"She wasn't the best of us," Natalie reasoned, "and she was getting older."

Augie, a year older than Clarissa, shuffled uncomfortably.

"Or maybe it was just getting a little crowded around here," Wilson suggested cynically. "Someone had to go to make room for the fair-haired boy."

Jax blanched.

"We don't know anything for sure," Kira jumped in. "Dr. Mako always does what's best for the institute, but nobody can be certain exactly what he's thinking and why."

"True that," said Wilson with a sneer in Jax's direction. "Anyway, it's not like we could look her up and ask her."

"What do you mean?" Jax demanded. "Why not?"

Wilson shrugged. "You're the big genius. You figure it out."

"Last year," Grace said timidly, "this kid Rory got bounced. About a month later, I was coming home from a tennis match, and I saw him on a subway platform. He definitely saw me — I'd swear to it. But he looked right through me."

"You can't be sure of that," Kira reminded her. "Maybe he's bitter because he washed out, and he was ignoring you."

"Or maybe when you leave this place, you leave without your memory," said Wilson. "Like cleaning out your desk. Only in this case, they clean out your head."

"But that can't happen!" Jax insisted. "Can it?"

"It happens to the Monopolies every day," Singh One pointed out.

"But with them, you're talking about a few hours," Jax argued. "Clarissa was here for, like, years!"

"It would take planning," Augie said thoughtfully. "A series of post-hypnotic suggestions that could be activated later. That's Ray's specialty. And who knows what Dr. Mako might be capable of?"

"He could have already implanted the groundwork for something like that in all of us," mused Natalie.

"Count on it," Wilson put in. "The doc's not the type to leave things up to chance."

"But Dr. Mako never bends *us*," Jax protested.

Tolerant chuckles and rolling eyes greeted this statement.

"Clueless!" spat Wilson.

Kira was gentler. "How many times a day do you use some form of the phrase, 'When you awaken, you will remember none of this'?"

Jax swallowed hard.

At the end of the long Saturday, Jax was on his way to the subway when a tug on his jacket spun him around on the sidewalk. There stood a hulking man, easily twice his weight.

"Daddy!" the man exclaimed in a basso voice that nevertheless sounded like baby talk. "I have to go to the bathroom!"

Shaken, Jax tried to keep on walking.

The man scrambled in front of him and blocked his way. "I have to *go*!" he insisted.

"Listen, mister, I'm not your daddy —"

To his horror, the big fellow clamped arms of steel

around him and squeezed hard. "C'mon, Daddy, quit kidding around! I have to go *really bad*!"

Jax's legs buckled under him, and he fell backward, drawing the big man on top of him. The guy easily weighed two hundred and fifty pounds — probably more!

"Jax?" All at once, the beautiful face of Ms. Samuels was peering down at him. "Are you all right? What's going on here?"

A ringtone sounded, very close. It must have been the man's phone. He rolled off of Jax and sat up on the pavement, his face a study in confusion. "What happened? Did I faint?"

Jax scrambled to his feet just in time to catch sight of two figures sprinting down East Sixty-Fifth Street, laughing and celebrating. Wilson and DeRon.

"Wow, kid, I'm sorry! Are you hurt?"

"I'm okay." Jax's eyes were on Ms. Samuels, who hadn't noticed the fleeing hypnos. The assistant director had relatively little mesmeric ability herself, but had been around Mako and Sentia long enough to recognize hypnotic mischief.

Jax had to admit that using the cell phone to break the subject out of his trance had been a brilliant touch. If you could bend a grown man to think a twelve-year-old kid was his daddy, it probably wasn't hard to get the guy to give you his number.

Ms. Samuels regarded Jax suspiciously. "Is there anything you want to tell me about this? Something Dr. Mako should know?"

Jax hesitated. Misuse of hypnotism was a very serious charge at Sentia. If it stuck, it would get both Wilson and DeRon kicked out of the institute. They were jerks, but he wasn't sure they deserved that.

"It was nothing," he said finally. "That guy must have had a dizzy spell."

12

The picture-in-picture image was sharper than Jax had ever seen it in his three weeks at Sentia. It was himself, from a range of seven feet, the exact distance between him and Mr. Marvin, a shabby homeless man, probably in his mid-fifties.

The subject's focus on Jax's eyes — now a deep aquamarine — was so intense that he was like a statue. His only motion was the rise and fall of his chest as he breathed.

Dr. Mako sat behind Jax, overseeing the process. Ordinarily, the director floated around the institute, dropping in on the occasional session. He had insisted, however, on supervising this hypnotism personally. "Keep him relaxed," Mako instructed. "Clear his mind of all thoughts."

"You're reclining on the softest feather bed in the world," Jax said quietly. "The material cradles you in total comfort."

The subject seemed to settle back on the hard wooden chair.

With the man deeply entranced, Jax risked a look at the director as if to say *What next?*

"Concentrate," Mako whispered. "Hold him in your power. Don't lose him."

Jax was a little confused. He couldn't lose this subject if he tried. The link was airtight, the PIP so vivid that it seemed as real as the room around him. It was like looking in a mirror.

This was the point where a staff member would usually tell him what to do to complete the exercise — induce an action or behavior. Last week, the Lancaster Singhs had convinced two subjects that they were chess masters, although neither had ever played the game. In spite of that, they had subsequently played a hard-fought match that was half checkers and half Parcheesi. Dr. Mako had called it inspired.

Jax had looked on with envy. How must it feel to have the great man heaping praise on you? He longed for it to be his turn.

This could be the day! I've never felt the connection stronger!

But first Mako had to give him something to *do*. Was the director waiting for him to come up with something on his own?

Am I blowing it?

A great weight of failure pressed down on him. He hadn't chosen Sentia, but now that he was here, washing out was unthinkable. No wonder he felt so depressed. He was a loser, alone, deserted, his beloved wife lost forever. . . .

Wife?

And then the image was upon him: a woman's face — dazzling smile, soft brown hair, upswept brows. She was laughing, which for some reason only made Jax sadder. All at once, the picture was fading, receding into a maelstrom of billowing dust and smoke. He actually reached out for her, in spite of the fact that he knew it was only a vision — some kind of hypnotic side effect. And anyway, it didn't do any good. She was gone.

The swirling mist faded to reveal a new picture: words engraved in marble, BELOVED WIFE AND MOTHER. . . .

A gravestone.

When Jax began to cry, it was convulsive — great wracking sobs that threatened to tear him open. Nothing in his twelve years came close to this shattering loss. It was all-consuming, a tragedy so overwhelming that it would be impossible to move beyond it. It was the end of the world.

Caught up in his weeping, he was only dimly aware of the moment he slid from the chair, sinking to his knees. When the mesmeric link broke, it brought no relief, only the disorienting sensation of waking from a terrible nightmare. The image was gone, but the horror was still there. He would never be whole again.

Even when Mr. Marvin had left the room and Jax was fully back to himself, the air of catastrophe surrounded him.

"I'm sorry," he quavered, still trembling. "What happened?"

"I should be the one apologizing to you," Dr. Mako

said gently. "I could try to describe this phenomenon to you. But the only way to truly understand it is to experience it firsthand."

"Phenomenon?" Jax managed.

"The mesmeric connection is a powerful coupling of two minds," the director explained gravely. "You are in control, but also vulnerable. When you 'see' through your subject's eyes, you've admitted a stranger's consciousness into your head. If the link goes on for too long, the subject's memories begin to leach into your brain. This can be like experiencing a lifetime of tragedy in a single moment."

"It was his wife, right?" Jax asked. "His wife died?"

Mako nodded. "To absorb — in an instant — the emotional highs and lows of a twenty-year marriage ending in catastrophe is not natural, especially for someone your age. You must learn to recognize when this is happening to you, and set up defenses against it. Or even bail out, if necessary. For a mind-bender, it's simple self-preservation."

"What happens if you don't? Or if you can't?"

"It's impossible to know. You might become hopelessly lost in the consciousness of another. Or perhaps the two minds will begin to meld. Either path will almost certainly lead to madness."

It was a sobering thought. He'd thought of hypnotism as a one-way operation — something to do to another person. It had never occurred to him that there was a flipside — that *he* might be in danger because of his subject.

"Thanks, Dr. Mako." He stood up to leave, and then turned. "How did she die?"

The director looked blank.

"Mr. Marvin's wife," Jax explained. "What happened to her?"

"It shouldn't matter to you," Mako replied. "You have to focus on your craft, not on the details of the people you mesmerize."

"But I could tell that he really loved her," Jax persisted. "She wasn't that old. Did she get sick?"

"This is weakness," Dr. Mako warned.

"It's just that I felt his sadness. No, it was more than that. *His* sadness was *my* sadness. We were one mind."

The director looked down at his notes and did not respond. Assuming that he was being dismissed, Jax started out the door.

"She died in 9/11," Dr. Mako said suddenly.

Jax froze halfway into the corridor.

"She went to work that morning and never came home. It was their wedding anniversary. It destroyed him." Dr. Mako regarded him critically. "Do you feel better now?"

"You were right," Jax said in a strangled voice. "It's worse when you know."

He stumbled out into the hallway, his face white. In his haste to get away from the memory that was not his, yet now somehow *was*, he bumped into Augie and Kira. A stack of books dropped from Kira's arms and hit the floor.

"Sorry," he mumbled, stooping to help gather them up.

She took in his red-rimmed eyes and ghastly countenance. "What's wrong?" Her glance shifted to the sight of the director leaving the room. "It was just you and Dr. Mako?" she asked sharply.

"It was terrible," Jax confessed. "Mr. Marvin's wife —"

"Well, poor you," she said coldly and stormed away.

Jax was mystified. "What was that for?"

"Dr. Mako left you stranded in the link," Augie concluded.

"It's like I lived a whole life in eight minutes."

The older boy nodded. "He only does it with the most promising hypnos. That's why Kira was upset. She was the last of us to get it. In her mind, she's being replaced."

"What's *she* got to worry about? She's the best of us by far!"

"It's possible our imperious leader doesn't think so anymore."

Jax appraised Augie, searching for signs that the seventeen-year-old was pulling his chain. Augie was a good hypnotist and a brilliant student, yet he lacked the imagination for jokes or even sarcasm.

Jax knew he was making progress at Sentia, but he was nowhere near Kira's level. Today was proof of that — he had very nearly lost himself in the mourning of a 9/11 widower. To a certain degree, it had actually happened. The ache of Mr. Marvin's calamity hadn't gone away. The connection of their minds ensured that Jax would always own a small amount of that pain.

He understood that his training had changed in a

fundamental way. Up until this point, his lessons had focused on the mechanics of hypnotism, and the possibilities.

Now it was time for him to learn about something new.

The risks.

13

Corrado's Pizza on Lexington Avenue was right around the corner from the institute. The mind-benders considered it their place, and there might have been some truth to that. Wilson bragged that he had once bent Corrado himself, demanding thinner crust and less oregano in the sauce. While no one could confirm whether or not this was true, the food was good, the service quick, and the prices affordable.

Jax ate there most Thursdays, when both his parents tended to work late, leaving him on his own for dinner. He was just enjoying his second slice when he became aware of that water-down-the-wrong-pipe feeling in his mind. It didn't alarm him anymore. He was used to it — a stirring in his brain, faint at first, but growing in intensity until it oozed all the way down his spine. He had long since learned to recognize the sensation that someone was trying to hypnotize him. Soon the random motion began to feel *directed*, like an intelligent force was vying for control.

His first instinct was to look around for somebody else from Sentia. Technically, the hypnos were forbidden to bend one another, but in reality, it happened a lot. Enforcing such a ban would be like trying to outlaw towel-snapping in a locker room. The Lancaster Singhs did more work on each other than on actual institute research. The two cousins knew just when to back off before the link became obvious to Ray or Ms. Samuels. As far as Jax could tell, they never risked it in front of the director himself.

Jax frowned. At the moment, he was the only one of Mako's young protégés in the shop.

His eyes fell on a slight, round-faced man in his sixties, with rosy cheeks and long gray hair tied back in a ponytail. His expression was so friendly, so nonthreatening that Jax scanned past him several times, certain that no hypnotic power could be coming from him. Yet the probing continued. Jax considered his other suspects. There was a lady at a corner table, lost in the depths of a thick paperback novel. A college-age girl sat slumped over her slice, seemingly fast asleep. Two men in suits were in a heated argument over a basketball game. It had to be the little guy, no question about it.

Well, Jax wasn't a novice anymore. At Sentia, he was working with Dr. Mako, the best in the business. He didn't have to be afraid of some plaid-shirted Grandpa Yokel.

Jax wielded his gaze like a weapon, transfixing the little man. The PIP image of himself came immediately, almost a flash. "Go away," Jax said quietly but very clearly. He was gratified to see the old guy get up and rush out of the pizzeria, ponytail bouncing.

Nice work, he commended himself, impressed by his skills. Too bad Dr. Mako hadn't been around to see it. That thought kept him content through his dinner, and he left Corrado's in an excellent mood.

"You pack quite a wallop, my young friend," came a voice from the storefront next door.

Jax wheeled. It was the little man who'd tried to hypnotize him. His eyes darkening through the blues toward purple, Jax tried again, focusing all his concentration on the target, just as Mako had taught him.

The man flinched, then grinned. "See what I mean? That's a real haymaker. I can always tell a fellow sandman."

Sandman? "Don't know what you're talking about, mister."

The old guy chuckled. "Sure, you do. Brain jockey, dream weaver, mind-bender, synapse surfer — whatever Elias Mako is calling us these days."

Jax hesitated. It was easy enough to accept that there were random people who had mesmeric power. Up until a few weeks ago, he had been one of them, bending strangers without even understanding what he was doing. But this old man was different. He knew about Mako *and* that Jax was connected to him. "I — I think you've got the wrong guy."

"Just because Mako treats his charm school like a top-secret operation doesn't make it one. All you have to do is stand next to the elevator and see who goes to the top three floors." The man grasped Jax's hand and shook it.

"Where are my manners? I'm Axel — Axel Braintree, president of the Sandman's Guild."

Jax was stunned. "There's a guild? Just how many hypnotists are out there?"

Braintree shrugged. "Could be millions. Most of them will never know their abilities exist. They're nothing to worry about — their power is too weak to make any difference. But someone like you, Jackson Opus, that's another tin of sardines. There are perhaps half a dozen sandmen on this earth with a gift that equals yours. If that many. For all I know, you're unique."

Jax bristled. "How do you know my name?"

"The guild takes an interest in Dr. Mako's Flying Circus. I like to find out all about his zombie army. To be honest, most of you are not very impressive. Generally, we sandmen are a lot more boring than people think. But when I did my research on you, needless to say, that really shingled my roof."

"Yeah, I know all about the Opuses," Jax said. "My dad doesn't have the power, though."

Braintree nodded wisely. "It skips a generation sometimes, and comes out even stronger the next time around."

"My father was hoping it just, you know, went away. He wasn't too happy when I got it."

"But surely he was expecting it," Braintree said with a frown. "After all, he *did* marry Monica Woodson."

"So what? Mom has nothing to do with this."

The old guy was amazed. "Not possible. Are you trying to tell me that your father didn't know the true identity of his wife-to-be?"

Jax was growing impatient. "He knew exactly who he was marrying! My mother!"

Braintree flushed with the effort of getting his point across. "Monica Woodson — Monica Opus — is a *Sparks*!"

"And?"

"If there's a clan with an even greater hypnotic legacy than the Opuses, it's the Sparks family!"

"No way!" Jax exploded. "My mother has no special powers at all! She can't even make the blender work! She didn't have a clue about Dad's family until Dr. Mako got him to confess."

"That's understandable. The Sparkses' mesmeric ability has eroded down through the generations. They were no less capable than the Opuses, but they were a different, wealthier breed — nobility, even royalty. It was said that an Opus would bend a butcher to get a free pork chop. Not so with the Sparks line. They were great sandmen, but to them, the gift was an art form, for entertainment and to do good works. A luxury, not a necessity. It might have been this difference that allowed their power to dissipate."

"You mean, like, use it or lose it?" Jax's head was spinning.

"You're a quick study," Braintree approved. "The Sparkses' gift might have disappeared entirely if a Sparks girl hadn't, by sheer random chance, married an Opus. And that makes you the nexus of the two most powerful bloodlines in the history of hypnotism."

Jax was silent for a long time. "Mom never mentioned a family named Sparks. And neither did Dr. Mako."

The round pink face turned grave. "I guarantee you that Dr. Mako knows everything I know and more. If he's withholding information, it's because he doesn't want you to realize just how special you might be. Watch out for him. He's a dangerous man."

"Oh, sure!" Jax exclaimed in outrage. "Dr. Mako *only* has his own institute, and hangs out with world leaders and movie stars, but I can't trust him. No, I have to trust some hobo who tried to hypnotize me in a pizza joint. How stupid do I look?"

Braintree was unflappable. "I know it's a lot to take in." He produced a business card and handed it to Jax:

He scribbled an address in the West Village onto the back. "The Sandman's Guild is having a meeting next Tuesday at eight o'clock. It might be an eye-opening experience for you — and that's quite a pair of eyes you've got, by the way. There were Opuses like that — green to purple in ten seconds. See you then."

He melted into the passing parade on Lexington Avenue, leaving Jax fuming in front of Corrado's.

Jax's mind sizzled. He wasn't going to any Sandman's meeting, that was for sure!

14

Maureen Samuels was a former Miss Nebraska who'd originally come to New York City to seek her fortune as a model. Despite her spectacular good looks, her hypnotic abilities always held her back. She seemed unfocused on the runway as she tried to make sense of PIP visions from spectators she'd unintentionally bent. Dr. Mako had rescued her from the fashion rat race and encouraged her to develop her mesmeric skills. Alas, her power as a mind-bender never lived up to its potential. And since she was unfit to be one of Sentia's hypnos, the director offered her a job running the place.

She also gave weekly lectures on the history of hypnotism. Jax always had trouble concentrating during these because a) it was pretty dull stuff, and b) every time he looked at Ms. Samuels for more than a few seconds, his mind went all foggy. He was embarrassed to admit that this had nothing to do with hypnotism. After more than a month at Sentia, you'd think he'd be used to how gorgeous she was. But then she'd turn a certain way, and he'd see her from an angle that he'd never noticed before, and it would start up again. The other boys had the same problem, with the possible exception of the Lancaster Singhs, one of whom always seemed to be mesmerized by the other. Wilson, too, seemed immune, or maybe he was too mean to show it.

The only thing that kept Jax reasonably alert was the name Opus, which dropped from those luscious lips on a regular basis. Dad didn't know the half of what his famous family had stuck their noses into over the years. Every walk of life seemed to have an Opus in the background, using hypnotic power for every purpose, from altering the course of nations to making a fast buck on the side. There was Cornelius Opus, the ambassador; and Lucas Opus, the spy; and Millicent Opus-Bourne, the audience-bending ballerina. Even when the name was von Kalben or Ivanov, sooner or later a connection to Somebody Opus would surface. Yet when the history books were written, and the world read about the Pony Express, the Russian Revolution, the invention of the telephone, or Wilt Chamberlain's hundred-point game, there was no mention of the Opus behind the scenes who'd helped make it happen.

But in today's lecture, the name that came up and rattled around Jax's head was not Opus. It was Sparks.

After being accosted by Axel Braintree, Jax had asked his mother if she knew of any relatives named Sparks. She'd looked so completely blank that he'd believed her. But according to Ancestry.com, there had been an aunt named Beatrice Sparks-Tremblay living in a castle in England in the early 1800s. The website hadn't offered much more information than that, but the castle part seemed to support what Braintree had said about the Sparks family being rich.

Dad had never heard of the Sparkses either, but his reaction was different. "My head explodes every time I think about my *own* wing-nut family. Don't ask me about somebody else's!"

It was pretty mind-blowing: Mom and Dad had met on a blind date at a roller rink. Uniting the two greatest mesmeric bloodlines in history had been the last thing on their minds. What were the odds?

Mom was in denial. "It's a coincidence. There must be dozens of old families named Sparks."

Poor Dad. He'd spent his whole childhood terrified that his parents were messing with his mind. Imagine his relief when he believed that the family talent had ended with his mother and father. Then one night he strapped on a pair of roller skates. . . .

Ashton Opus was having a lot of flashbacks to his youth these days. "I washed the car every Saturday. I used to look forward to it all week. I think I got into the car business because I loved taking care of those old sedans." His brow clouded. "Or maybe your grandparents were just too cheap to go to the car wash. . . ."

None of these conversations took place head-on. Dad now preferred to address Jax from the side. He was paranoid that his son might be hypnotizing him, just as his parents had. Even when they had no choice but to face each other — over a chessboard, for example — Mr. Opus focused on a spot over Jax's left shoulder. How messed up was that? His own father wouldn't look at him.

These were the thoughts that roiled in Jax's head when Ms. Samuels spoke the name Braintree had supplied and Mom had denied.

"Sparks?" he choked out.

The assistant director frowned at him from the front of the lecture room. "Sparks used to be a very common name in hypnotic circles. In the eighteenth and nineteenth centuries, Sparks hypnotists contributed more to the refinement of our craft than anyone else. They never asked for reward, nor did they accept one. It was the scandal of the family when Dr. Franz Mesmer began to use the gift to make money in eighteenth-century Paris."

"Mesmer!" Wilson whistled. "The big dog was a Sparks?"

There was no brighter star in hypnotic history than Franz Mesmer. Mesmerism was named after him. Plenty of famous people *happened* to be mind-benders, from Winston Churchill to Eminem. Mesmer was more than that. He was famous *for* his hypnotic abilities. If Mom really was a Sparks, her pedigree might be even more top-shelf than Dad's.

"He was born a Sparks, but they disowned him," Ms. Samuels replied. "Mesmer is considered the father of our art. But those on the inside know he was just another huckster. That kind of behavior might have been acceptable among the Opuses, or the Desais, or even the mysterious Petrocellis. But the Sparkses would never tolerate it."

Kira raised her hand. "What happened to the Sparks family? Are they still active in the hypnotic community?"

The assistant director shook her head. "Their talents became diluted, and their descendants lost the power. What's happened to them is anybody's guess."

If you'd bothered to check the chiropractic clinics, Jax couldn't help reflecting, *you could have gotten your neck cracked or your spine realigned by one!*

Did Ms. Samuels know? Did Dr. Mako?

He thought back to Braintree's words: *Dr. Mako knows everything I know and more. If he's withholding information, it's because he doesn't want you to realize just how special you might be.*

Oh, sure. Believe some old geezer with a gray ponytail over a respected scientist.

And yet . . .

Jax was 99 percent sure Axel Braintree was full of baloney. But 99 wasn't quite the same as 100.

There was a way to get to the bottom of this. The Sandman's Guild was meeting tonight. Braintree had written the address on his card.

The two words came to Jax as if in a hypnotic vision: *DON'T GO.* Hadn't enough crazy stuff happened already? Did he really think Braintree, of all people, would bring order to the chaos?

Yet on the subway that night, Jax wasn't even surprised when he abandoned his train in favor of the shuttle to the West Side lines. The 1 would drop him just a few blocks from the address on the card.

Jackson Opus was going to a meeting.

15

Jax stared from the sign to the business card in his hand, and back again. This was definitely the right address. Inside, customers stuffed bundles of clothes into industrial-size washers and dryers. A few sat on benches, reading magazines and fiddling with phones, waiting impatiently for loads to finish. He checked his watch: 8:10. There was no meeting going on, and definitely no meeting of hypnotists.

Why would Axel Braintree browbeat him into attending a gathering of the Sandman's Guild and then send him to the wrong place? Was Braintree such a flake that he honestly couldn't remember the location of his own meeting? Maybe the whole thing was just a joke. But if so, there was nobody around to enjoy the payoff. Jax looked up and down Seventh Avenue. No sign of the old guy with the ponytail.

Jax watched as a young, twitchy man entered E-Z Wash carrying no laundry bag or basket, his hands jammed inside the pouch of his hoodie. Glancing furtively over his shoulder, he lifted the lid and peered inside one of the washers, only to be shouted away by a lady with a toy poodle on her hip. He spun around, raising his arms in a gesture of innocence, and darted down a back hall. He was followed a few minutes later by a very tall woman in a voluminous trench coat. She made no pretense of being a customer, sweeping by the machines and disappearing in the bend of the rear corridor.

Self-consciously, Jax stepped inside and made his way to the back. There was no sign except a small message board that read OF ICE in uneven magnetic letters. There were two doors off the short hall. One provided access to a Stone Age bathroom. Jax could hear muffled voices coming from behind the other. It was open a crack, and he pressed his face to the jamb to peer inside.

He spotted Braintree's pink face and gray ponytail almost immediately. About fifteen people sat in a circle on folding bridge chairs. Jax wasn't sure what he'd expected a professional organization of hypnotists to look like — magicians, maybe; psychics, shamans, or even sorcerers. But the collection of individuals in Braintree's "guild" seemed closer to the crowd you'd encounter hanging out overnight at a bus station than a group that shared a rare and powerful supernatural talent. A few had come straight from work in suits and business attire. There was a mom who carried a sleeping infant in a BabyBjörn. In general, though, this seemed like a scruffy crew. The clothes were ill-matched and ragged; shoes were scuffed and worn. Ripped jeans, unshaven faces.

". . . I haven't bent anyone for seventeen weeks," a stocky thirty-something man with bright red hair announced to a smattering of applause.

"Excellent, Ivan," Braintree approved.

"Except my landlady," Ivan finished.

The ovation died abruptly.

"Well, I had to. If she doesn't believe my apartment is rent controlled, I won't be able to afford to live there anymore."

"Using your power to pay less for something is the same as using it to swindle or steal," the old man lectured, ponytail bobbing earnestly.

"I'm not going to Hoboken," Ivan stated flatly.

"We all have a gift," Braintree lectured. "But we have to resist the temptation to use our abilities for personal gain. There's a deeper satisfaction that comes from making an honest living. Look at Evelyn. She's waitressing now."

The tall woman in the trench coat stood up. "I got fired," she admitted, shamefaced. "There were . . . complaints."

"Hypnotism isn't going to keep you from spilling soup on somebody," Ivan commiserated.

She shook her head. "It wasn't that. It was my tips. They were . . . large."

Braintree sighed. "You didn't."

"People are so *cheap*," she complained. "I just made a little suggestion. Fifteen percent — is that too much to ask for? It's not my fault that one guy signed over his life-insurance policy. What kind of idiot tacks a life-insurance policy onto a restaurant tab? What kind of idiot brings life insurance to a restaurant in the first place?"

"There's no such thing as a little suggestion," the old man explained patiently. "Hypnotizing for a penny is no different than hypnotizing for millions."

"In that case," the mom put in sourly, "I should just go back to Wall Street."

"Wall Street is the worst hotbed of misguided mesmerism anywhere!" Braintree warned. "Don't risk it! You have a wonderful family. It's what you and your husband dreamed of."

"What he *thought* he dreamed of, anyway," she amended.

The old man raised his arms to quell a babble of conversation. "Sandmen —"

"We're not all sand*men*," Evelyn put in. "I happen to be a sand*woman*. In fact, I move that we change our name to the Sand*person*'s Guild."

"We've been through this before, Evelyn. We consider everyone — male or female — an equal sandman. Plus, we're a support group, not the Loyal Order of Water Buffaloes. We don't make motions. We're just here to help one another grapple with a special ability that can be really tempting to abuse sometimes."

"And for the free donuts," added a voice near the back.

"They cut out donuts last November," the mom said mournfully.

In the groundswell of discontented murmuring, two sandmen got up and headed for the exit.

Braintree watched in exasperation as his numbers dwindled — until he noticed the newcomer outside the door. Jax felt the familiar stirring, soon to become a tugging. The president of the Sandman's Guild was locked onto his gaze.

"I believe we have a visitor."

Sheepishly, Jax stepped into the room. "I was in the neighborhood. . . ."

Braintree rushed over and escorted him to an empty seat. "Jackson Opus!" To the others, he put in, "You recognize the name, of course — Opus?"

"Call me Jax. Uh — I hope I'm not interrupting anything important."

"Welcome, welcome! Jax has been working with Dr. Mako uptown. I invited him here so he could see the other side of the manhole cover."

The other side of the manhole cover was not pretty. While Sentia was a respected organization supported by some of the wealthiest, most accomplished, and most famous figures in the world, the Sandman's Guild was a ragtag coffee klatch minus the coffee. The contrast could not have been more obvious. The institute occupied the top three floors of a beautiful building in the most expensive part of New York City. The guild met in the back room of a Laundromat. Dr. Mako and Ms. Samuels could have shared the cover of *GQ* magazine; Axel Braintree looked like an ex-hippie turned Walmart greeter. Most glaring of all, Sentia was a research lab, dedicated to harnessing mesmeric power for the good of all humanity. The guild was a gaggle of two-bit con artists trying to kick the habit of bending unsuspecting marks into falling for sleazy scams.

That began to sink in as the various members introduced themselves. Ivan Marcinko was a former electronics salesman who was fired for being too good at his job. He had a knack for convincing customers to buy expensive TVs they didn't want or need. It was the next-day returns that did him in. Evelyn Lolis used to make her living winning beauty contests until her pictures in the newspaper elicited too many letters of complaint accusing the panel of either bias or blurred vision. The judges were easy to hypnotize, but it was impossible to reach everybody who read the paper.

There was a bank teller who persuaded depositors to leave with a little less money than they'd withdrawn, and a jury consultant who was having entirely too much to do with the outcome of trials. There was a panhandler who was getting diamond rings and Rolex watches tossed into his hat, and a ninety-eight-pound arm wrestler who had never lost a match.

Even Braintree himself was a former abuser of his gift — and not for small potatoes. He had actually spent time in prison for art theft. He would bend museum security into not noticing that he was stuffing paintings and small sculptures under a voluminous raincoat. Even in jail, he'd managed to gain favors and privileges by mesmerizing the guards. At his parole hearing, he'd hypnotized the entire board into granting him early release.

"Don't you see?" The old man's face was even pinker than usual in his sincerity. "I thought the rules didn't apply to me because of my power over people's minds. Even when I was caught and punished, I found a way to weasel out of it through hypnotism. I was young and foolish, and I was going to go back into society to make the same mistakes all over again."

"How did you stop yourself?" Jax asked, interested in spite of the discomfort these revelations were bringing him.

"On the bus home from prison, I tried to bend the driver into letting me on without paying. That's how arrogant I was — I wouldn't hand over fifty cents to avoid doing what had gotten me arrested in the first place. But it didn't work. The driver was a fellow sandman — and a powerful one. Before I knew it, I was dropping coins in the fare box happily. It seemed like the most natural thing in the world! When I was back to myself, I asked him how come a guy with his gift was driving a bus. He could be making millions in Vegas or on Wall Street, playing it 99 percent straight, beating the odds with just a little bit of hypnotism. And he clicked two quarters from his coin belt and held them out to me. 'You want a free ride? You think it's really free?'

"In that moment," Braintree went on, "I saw what my future would be if I took that money. Fifty lousy cents, but it was the difference between living a decent life and being a crook forever. It's been thirty years since that day, and I'm proud to announce that I haven't bent a penny out of anyone."

The guild broke into spontaneous applause. Jax couldn't help noticing that there were a lot of moist eyes in the room, not to mention more than a few shamed expressions. Maybe Axel Braintree had been on the wagon for three decades, but some members could count the time since their last transgressions in hours, and possibly minutes.

"But what does this have to do with Dr. Mako?" Jax probed. "He's not like that at all. The goal of Sentia is to make the world a better place."

"That's what he *wants* you to think," Braintree corrected.

"That's what *everybody* thinks!" Jax insisted. "Do you have any idea how many big shots and celebrities support Sentia? When my family first met Dr. Mako, guess who was coming out of his office while we were going in: Senator Trey Douglas — a guy who could be our next president! If he trusts Dr. Mako, why don't you?"

"Senator Douglas is a politician, not a sandman."

"Look, I get it," said Jax, becoming annoyed. "If you guys didn't have your little support-group meetings, you'd be out there bending blackjack dealers and buying iPads for a nickel by hypnotizing the clerks at the Apple store. Well, just because *you* have to wrestle with the temptation to rip people off doesn't mean Dr. Mako does!"

The old man sighed heavily. "Let's assume for a minute that you're right. That Dr. Mako is telling the truth, and he intends to use the power only for good. What would that 'good' be, exactly?"

"Well . . ." Jax drew a blank. At the institute, the hypnos made their subjects jump, laugh, cry, and scratch nonexistent itches. It was hard to see how humankind would benefit from that. Of course, it was just training, to prepare for the real thing — which no one had ever spoken much about.

Exactly what *was* the real thing?

"I don't know," Jax admitted finally. "But it seems to me that if you can use hypnotism to influence a really bad gangster or an evil dictator into becoming a better person, that would be good for the world, wouldn't it?"

"It would," Braintree agreed. "If it worked. Which it wouldn't. There's no sandman alive who can change what's in somebody's heart. You can make a gangster call off a hit. But if you try to convince a violent man that killing is wrong, it may work for a day, a week, even a month. Sooner or later, though, the suggestion will wear off."

"Maybe that's the whole point of Sentia," Jax argued. "To develop a new approach. You look at the power as something that has to be controlled to keep it from being abused. And that's fine — I can see you're doing a lot of great things around the — uh — Laundromat. But Dr. Mako sees it as something wonderful, like the invention of the wheel or the discovery of electricity. Something that can revolutionize the world. Just because we haven't figured out how to do that yet doesn't mean we should stop trying."

Braintree regarded him with a new respect. "You're a smart kid. You're not going to rejigger what you believe on my say-so. But that should go for Dr. Mako as well. Do you honestly believe that he has no idea that you carry Sparks blood as well as Opus? Why would he keep this from you? Do you think he's afraid to let you find out how powerful you may be?"

"Me? Compared to Dr. Mako? I don't even come up to his ankles."

"My point exactly," Braintree jumped in. "You don't have the experience to make sense of everything that's going on at that institute. Let *me* be your guide. Tell me everything that's happening over there, and I can interpret it for you."

Jax was outraged. "That's not you being a guide; that's *me* being a *spy*!"

"If you want to put it that way," the guild leader acknowledged. "But if Mako's as clean as you say, then he can stand the inspection."

Jax stood up. "I'm sorry I came here. You're nothing but a bunch of cheap con men. And you've got the *nerve* to dump all over Dr. Mako, who has devoted his life to New York City education and is an insp —" He caught himself. "Well, he's a better person than all of you put together!"

He stormed out through the Laundromat into the darkening streets of Greenwich Village.

16

Kira Kendall recognized the young woman in the surgical scrubs immediately. Miss Ventnor stood in the line of volunteers waiting for the service elevator. She was paying her way through nursing school by volunteering for every focus group and clinical trial in the city. But it was not her life story that rang a bell with the young hypno.

Miss Ventnor was practically impossible to bend.

It was still a painful memory for Kira. She had never failed Dr. Mako before. But the nurse-to-be was a brick wall. No reflected image. No mental link. Zero.

The director had told her not to worry. "Our Miss V. is a very tough nut to crack."

"Even by you?"

He had smiled. "My gift is quite modest. I consider myself more a scientist than a virtuoso. But a mind-bender must experience subjects of all levels of resistance, since that is what you'll encounter in the real world."

Kira hadn't seen the nursing student around Sentia for months.

"Have any of you guys tried to hypnotize Miss Ventnor?" she asked the others in the lounge.

"You mean Unbendable?" Singh Two asked.

"Has anybody ever reached her?" asked Kira.

"I was close once," Augie volunteered. "For just a second, I got that flicker of the link. Then it was gone. I came up empty after that."

"Loser." Wilson snorted.

"Like you could do better," Singh One returned. "I'll bet they never even gave you a crack at her."

"The doc doesn't waste my talent on a lost cause," Wilson growled.

"You might be getting your chance today," DeRon pointed out. "They didn't bring her in to shampoo the rugs."

"Good point," said Kira. "Who's she here for?"

The hypnos took stock of themselves. It wasn't long before they realized who was absent from the lounge.

"Dopus?" sneered Wilson. "No way!"

"I don't know," Kira mused aloud. On the surface, Jax was inexperienced and timid. He had a knack for bending subjects quickly, but often lost his way once he had them under. Dr. Mako gave him a lot of attention, which might have been because his last name was Opus. That carried a lot of weight in the hypnotic world. But real talent? The jury was still out.

She left the lounge, letting the door slam shut behind her. What was the point of inviting Miss Ventnor back to Sentia except to face the institute's latest rising star?

Two experiment rooms were empty; a third was being cleaned. That meant the action was probably in Lab 1, which had a formal viewing gallery. All the important sessions took place there.

She let herself into the observation booth, noting that Dr. Mako, Ms. Samuels, Ray Finklemeyer, and all the senior Sentia staff were present. Through the glass she could see Miss Ventnor one-stepping across the room as if she were on a tightrope, arms outstretched for balance.

Kira did not have to guess at the identity of the hypno who had bent the unbendable subject.

Jackson Opus.

The surge of emotion shocked her — and shamed her, because she knew she had no right to feel such resentment. How many times had Dr. Mako told them that they had no more control over the strength of their gift than they had over their height or blood type? It was not her fault that Jax could hypnotize Miss Ventnor and she couldn't. She couldn't dunk a basketball either. Or fly.

Then why did this hurt so much?

She'd always accepted the argument when it came to explaining why she could do certain things Wilson, or Grace, or Augie couldn't. They'd all been at Sentia longer than she had. To them it must have seemed as if she'd parachuted out of nowhere and landed ahead of them in line.

It's good for the institute, she'd told herself to deflect the sting of their glares.

Kira believed in the institute 100 percent. She believed in Dr. Mako.

This had to be good for the institute, too.

So why did it seem so different now?

Because I'm the one on the outside looking in?

In Lab 1, Miss Ventnor was now doing the tango with an imaginary partner, to music only she could hear.

"Impressive," commented Ms. Samuels. "Do you think he could be the one?"

Dr. Mako nodded with satisfaction. "We'll soon see."

The change was subtle, but Jax couldn't miss it. Suddenly, all the Sentia staff knew his name, even the cleaning crew. Whispered conversations broke out wherever he went. He spent more and more time with Dr. Mako himself. There was an air of expectancy, like something big was coming. It was exciting, but also terrifying in a way. It was pretty obvious that, sooner or later, Jax was going to have to produce, to deliver. And he had absolutely no idea what was about to be asked of him.

He had spent the past two months squeezing his way into the unwelcoming group of hypnos. Now he found himself ostracized again, not because he was the new guy but because he had become the chosen one. Kira would barely look in his direction, and Grace and the Lancaster Singhs were tight-lipped in his presence. Wilson had carved a voodoo doll from a bar of soap and hung it on a string from the bulletin board in the lounge. On its chest was tacked a note: *DOPUS ON A ROPUS.*

On Saturday morning, Jax entered Lab 3 and was surprised to find a large video camera on a tripod across the table where the subject should have been. He looked questioningly from Dr. Mako to Ray, who was crouched at the viewfinder.

"A new approach," the director supplied. "We've decided to record you, so we can fine-tune your technique."

Jax was still in the dark. "Record me doing what? Where's the subject?"

"The camera is the subject," Ray told him.

"Obviously, you can't bend a piece of technology," Dr. Mako explained, "but it's important that you proceed as if there were a living, breathing person sitting across from you. It's more useful than a live hypnotism, since I'll have the recording to review multiple times, and not have to rely on my notes."

Jax was uncertain. "What do I say to it? Do I tell it to act like a toaster?"

The director chuckled. "I'd like you to employ a post-hypnotic suggestion. This is different than convincing a subject he is climbing a mountain, or skating, or wrestling a bear. A post-hypnotic suggestion is *delayed*. For example, you might say, 'When you hear the words *pot roast*, you will do twenty push-ups.' "

Jax nodded. He had never used post-hypnotic suggestion before, but there was always a lot of talk about it around Sentia. It was a very powerful tool, since the subject didn't have to be under when the payoff occurred. The reaction could take place hours, days, weeks, sometimes months after the suggestion was implanted. The trigger didn't even have to be a word. It could be a sound, or a picture, or even a gesture — like the pitcher in the

1932 World Series who'd been bent to throw a straight fastball over the center of home plate when Babe Ruth pointed at center field with his bat. It was a post-hypnotic suggestion that had enabled the Bambino to hit that historic home run.

The Lancaster Singhs were masters of the post-hypnotic suggestion in their ongoing hypno-battle. Every so often, one of the pair would do something wild and unpredictable, like tap-dancing on a cafeteria table, or stripping down to tighty whities and reciting the Gettysburg Address. And everyone knew that a long-embedded trigger word had come up in conversation.

"Since this is your first time," Dr. Mako went on, "I'll provide a trigger for you — a police siren. And the required action at that time will be to stand at attention and salute for thirty seconds. Remember, none of this is going to happen in reality. It's purely so we can judge the quality of your work on the recording."

It was unsettling to face not an actual person, but a camera, especially one so close that it seemed like the lens was a black hole about to swallow him. Jax caught a glimpse of Mako's monitor. The shot was so tight that it was all eyes — not quite purple yet, but a turbulent blue that betrayed his discomfort. He took a deep breath, determined to justify the director's faith in him. Dr. Mako wanted this, so Jax intended to ace it.

"Rolling," Ray reported.

Jax forced the camera from his mind and convinced himself that he was looking across the table at one of

Sentia's most pliable subjects, Ms. North Carolina, perhaps, or Mr. Pennsylvania.

"Relax . . ." he said quietly. "Look into my eyes . . . clear your mind . . . you are very comfortable . . . very happy . . ." He blinked, startled, when a PIP image appeared. How could that come from a camera, which had no mind for him to link with? Was it just a reflection from the lens? The vision of himself seemed to be framed, like a picture.

He soldiered on. "Now you are content and at ease. When I clap my hands, you'll be awake, feeling wonderful. You will remember nothing of this. But" — he paused, as he would with a live subject — "the next time you hear a police siren, you will come to attention in a salute, which you will hold for thirty seconds." He wasn't sure whether Dr. Mako wanted him to or not, since you couldn't wake up a camera, but he went through the whole routine, finishing with a sharp clap.

"Excellent," the director approved. He signaled to Ray to stop filming. "Now let's run that back."

"Sure thing, boss." The cameraman fiddled with controls to call up the recording. All at once, he leaped to his feet and snapped to a rigid military salute.

It was only then that they heard the police siren in the street outside the institute.

Jax was thunderstruck. "He's *bent*! I hypnotized him through the camera!"

Dr. Mako wore a triumphant smile. "It's not as if it's the first time your gift has touched our Ramolo. He does a very creditable chicken, I'm told."

"But he wasn't looking at *me*!" Jax persisted. "He only saw me through the lens! And the image I got — it was framed like the viewfinder!"

"You're very powerful, Jackson."

"Yeah — face-to-face! Ray was just looking at a *monitor*!" Another thought occurred to Jax. "Does that mean the recording can hypnotize, too?"

"No one has ever had the ability to hypnotize remotely," the director lectured. "Surely Ms. Samuels has taught you that."

"I know, but what's a viewfinder?" Jax persisted. "A screen! The one that bent Ray is no different than the screen of any TV or computer or phone!"

"I wish I had an answer for you," Dr. Mako admitted. "Hypnotism is not an exact science like chemistry or physics. We know that electricity is the movement of charged particles, and that light is made up of photons. But nobody truly understands the nuts and bolts of how mesmeric power is transmitted."

At that moment, Ray broke out of his salute. As if nothing had happened, he ejected the memory card and offered it to Dr. Mako. "Where do you want this, boss?"

"Shouldn't we watch it?" Jax queried. "You know, to make sure it came out okay?"

The director accepted the chip and tucked it into the pocket of his custom-tailored suit. "I saw it live on my monitor. It's perfect. Excellent work."

Another siren sounded outside, and Ray whipped into his formal salute.

Dr. Mako smiled. "I suppose I should have chosen

something that doesn't happen so frequently in New York City."

Jax looked embarrassed. "I haven't learned how to undo the suggestion yet."

"Oh, I'll take care of that," the director assured him. He looked over at the Amazing Ramolo, standing ramrod straight. "That's quite a fine salute. I wonder if Ray was ever in the army."

11

Tommy slammed his locker shut and turned to his friend. "You should listen to yourself, Opus. All you do is complain. At least you got picked for something. The last time I got picked for something? Third grade. Hall monitor. Got so nervous I threw up, slipped in my own barf, and broke my wrist."

"You don't know what it's like," Jax said. "My dad won't look at me because he's afraid of being bent. My mother's ticked off at Dad because he never told her about his family. And both of them would hit the roof if they knew about the night I went to the West Village to meet with sandmen."

They started down the hall toward science class. "If I could hypnotize people, I wouldn't be cooling my heels in any Laundromat," Tommy grumbled. "I'd be out there using my magic powers. It would be Christmas twenty-four-seven."

"That's the one thing the Sandman's Guild got right," Jax countered. "It's not good to get everything you want. That's what those guys tried to do, and their lives went bad because of it. Half of them did time; they've lost their families, their homes; and now they're breaking their necks trying to kick the habit."

"You sound like my mother," Tommy said sourly. "If you were a real friend, you'd be tossing a little of that alakazam my way."

"The power isn't transferable."

"You could get Mrs. Baker to find a few extra points in that math test," Tommy wheedled. "Maybe bump me up to a C-minus."

"That's exactly the kind of thing that lands you in the Sandman's Guild," Jax warned.

"What about Carol Ann Darby?" Tommy persisted.

"What about her?"

"You could hypnotize her to think I'm hot. And cool — not in the temperature sense, I mean —"

"Never!" Jax exclaimed. "Even the sandmen wouldn't stoop that low! It was lesson number one in Hypno-Ethics class!"

"What's so bad about it?" Tommy challenged. "Bringing two people together. It's like an online dating site."

Jax was disgusted. "First off, it's sleazy. Second, it doesn't really work. Sooner or later, it always wears off. Here's a crazy thought: If you want Carol Ann to be into you, don't act like a dork every time she walks into the room."

"Thanks for being so helpful. You're a pal."

They took their seats and riffled through their lab books to today's experiment. A group of girls sat down on the other side of the room, Carol Ann among them. Her eyes met Jax's briefly, and for an instant he toyed with the idea of how easy it would be to bend her. Not to make her fall madly in love with Tommy. Just to make her appreciate him a little, maybe think he was funny, or something.

Of course, he could be kicked out of Sentia for something like that.

At the next desk, Tommy was folding his homework into an elaborate paper airplane. Jax elbowed him in the ribs, and shook his head no. But his friend was not to be discouraged. He was going to get Carol Ann to notice him or die trying.

With an artistic flick of the wrist, he launched his creation into flight. An updraft took it across the room, where it bumped the wall and began sailing back to him like a boomerang. He was about to pluck it triumphantly out of the air when a large hand snatched it away from his grasp, crumpled it up, and tossed it in the nearest wastebasket. The teacher, Mr. Morrison.

"Hey, that was my homework!" Tommy said plaintively.

The whole class laughed.

Carol Ann and her friends were rolling their eyes as Tommy rummaged through the trash to come up with his paper. There must have been food in there because the page was grease-stained as he attempted to smooth it out. This got a round of applause. Tommy took a bow, smearing his T-shirt in the process.

If he's trying to get Carol Ann to notice him, he's doing great. If he wants her to like *him, then not so much.*

A thought occurred to Jax. He couldn't bend Carol Ann into loving Tommy. But would it be so terrible to use a *little* hypnotism to boost his friend's confidence? Nothing fancy, just a bit of extra self-assurance so the poor kid wouldn't think he had to be a clown to get a girl's attention. It was for Tommy's own good, after all. Even Axel Braintree couldn't argue with that.

One problem: Jax hadn't been able to bend Tommy before. But surely it was worth another try.

Tommy was in his seat again now, dabbing at the ketchup stain with a wadded-up Kleenex. Jax gave him the stare with both barrels.

He ratcheted his gaze up to full power. Thanks to his Sentia training, his mesmeric skills were so focused that he could usually rouse a PIP image in a matter of seconds. But to Tommy, the vivid blues and purples of the hypnotist's eyes were bland shades of gray. He misinterpreted the stare as disapproval for the paper-airplane incident, and fired back an *it-wasn't-my-fault* shrug.

Jax soldiered on. "You are a cool and happening guy," he said in a low voice. "You don't need to act like an idiot to get a girl to like you. . . ."

"What are you talking about, Opus?" Tommy whispered back. "Even *I* don't think I'm cool."

A PIP image opened up in front of him.

That's impossible! Tommy isn't hypnotized!

Remembering the incident with the lunch lady, he looked around the lab to see if anyone had ended up in the line of fire by mistake. All eyes were on Mr. Morrison, who had begun lecturing. No one was focused on Jax with that vacant, expectant look.

Yet the vision persisted, growing more vivid.

Who did I bend?

According to Dr. Mako, it was impossible to generate the image without a hypnotized subject.

Am I so wrapped up in Sentia that I don't know what I'm looking at anymore?

The picture began to come into focus. It was Jax in extreme close-up — already illogical, since the subject would have to be sitting in his lap for this point-blank view. Yet those were his eyes, his forehead, the bridge of his nose. . . .

In that instant, Jax knew with absolute certainty what he was looking at.

18

It was the *video* — the one that had hypnotized Ray during filming!

Someone, somewhere, was watching that recording and getting bent. And the blowback was coming to Jax, miles away.

I was right! If an accomplished mind-bender like Ray can be mesmerized through a viewfinder, the same thing could happen to anyone watching that clip!

It was a major discovery! He had to tell Dr. Mako!

"Mr. Opus." The teacher's sarcastic voice penetrated Jax's swirling thoughts. "Are you having a seizure, or do you need to go to the bathroom?"

"Dude, you're bouncing like a Ping-Pong ball," Tommy hissed.

"I — I gotta go!" He was up and out of the lab like a shot. The PIP was still dead center in his field of vision, so it was a miracle he made it to the bathroom without falling flat on his face or running full tilt into a wall.

He locked himself in a stall and waited, hyperventilating, for the vision to clear. It did eventually, but that did nothing to restore his calm. Trembling, he fumbled for his cell phone and dialed Sentia.

"It's Jackson Opus." He gasped. "I need to talk to Dr. Mako right away!"

"Dr. Mako's in a closed session," the receptionist informed him.

"Oh, for sure I know that!" Jax exclaimed. *He's showing someone my video — and he doesn't know the effect it's having!*

As usual, getting through to the director was like calling the Vatican and asking to speak to the Pope. Eventually, when Jax would not be denied, they bounced his call to Ms. Samuels.

"Jax — what's so urgent that it can't wait until this afternoon?"

Breathlessly, Jax panted out what had just happened to him and his theory as to why. "Don't you see? It should be impossible for me to have that vision unless I've bent somebody. But I *haven't*! It must be coming from the video."

Ms. Samuels was her usual unflappable self. "I'll try to get your message to Dr. Mako, but I can't guarantee anything. He's absolutely booked solid, and he's asked not to be interrupted."

"Yeah, because he's showing people *my* recording! And it's hypnotizing them!"

"Calm down," she soothed. "I'll see you in a few hours. There's nothing we can do now."

The rest of the day was a blur. Who could concentrate on Robert Frost or the Stamp Act when there was something going on that even Elias Mako didn't understand? The director had said it outright: *No one has ever been able to hypnotize remotely.* Yet that was exactly what had just taken place!

By the time Ms. Samuels greeted Jax at Sentia after school, Dr. Mako was out of the office at "important meetings."

"More important than *this*?" Jax demanded.

"I gave him your message, and he's looking into it," she told him. "He doesn't want you jumping to any conclusions."

Jax thought his head was going to explode. "What other conclusion could there possibly be?"

The supermodel features relaxed into a sympathetic smile. "Dr. Mako's on it. That's all we can ask for."

School had been hard enough, but to sit through History of Hypnotism when hypnotic history was being made right inside his head was pure torture. Who cared about the lost first draft of *The Lord of the Rings* in which Gandalf was a mind-bender, not a wizard? Who cared about the Gestapo interrogators who'd used mesmerism during World War II? The most important piece of news was breaking *now* — if Dr. Mako would bother to listen to him!

"Of course, no one's a fan of the Nazis," Ms. Samuels was saying, "but those officers with hypnotic power could avoid the use of less humane methods, like torture —"

"It's happening!" Jax exclaimed suddenly as the vision reappeared. As before, it was an extreme close-up of his eyes framed by a screen. Louder, *"It's happening!"*

Ms. Samuels tried to stare him into silence, but he was not to be denied.

"I need Dr. Mako *right now*!"

A foot kicked his chair from behind. "Can it, Dopus," came Wilson's voice. "Nobody cares what you need."

The vision was solidifying before his eyes, half blinding him. He rose unsteadily.

"Sit down, Jax," Ms. Samuels said gently.

"I'm going to find him!" He stumbled out of the seminar and began flinging doors open up and down the hall.

In one lab, Kira wheeled around in her chair, breaking her link with Mr. Kentucky. "You can't barge in here like that!"

"Where's Dr. Mako?" Jax insisted.

"Out!"

Jax was heading for Lab 1 when a flying tackle cut the legs out from under him. Wilson picked him up by the scruff of the collar. "Got him!"

"Bring him to my office," Ms. Samuels called back.

Jax struggled to break the iron grip. "Let go!"

"Please." Wilson sneered. "Put up a fight. This is turning into a really great day."

He sounded so genuinely thrilled that Jax came back to himself. Nothing would have pleased the bully more than a ready-made excuse to mash Jax to a pulp.

By the time Jax took the seat opposite Ms. Samuels's desk, the PIP had disappeared.

"Thank you, Wilson," she said. "Give my apologies to the group. I'll return to the seminar in a few minutes."

"I'm not making this up," Jax told her once Wilson was gone.

"I believe you," she acknowledged. "Yet you're going to have to keep it to yourself until Dr. Mako has time to discuss it with you."

"*Where*'s Dr. Mako?" Jax demanded. "I can't deal with this on my own."

The assistant director hesitated a moment. "This is just between you and me, agreed? Dr. Mako is helping Senator Douglas with his campaign. If he wins the New York primary, the nomination will be his. It's really exciting."

"I thought Dr. Mako was interested in hypnotism, not politics."

"He's interested in both," she soothed. "To have one of our supporters holding high office would be a fantastic boost to the good work we do here."

And Jax had to agree. The question remained: *How long would it be before he could get to the bottom of what was happening to him?*

19

The next vision came while Jax was having breakfast the following morning. It was so unexpected that he drew in a sharp breath and inhaled a mouthful of Raisin Bran. His father rushed over and began pounding him on the back.

Mr. Opus took his son's face in his hands and peered anxiously into his eyes — until he remembered and glanced quickly away. Even with Jax choking, he couldn't risk placing himself in the line of fire of the old family talent.

"You okay?" he tossed over his shoulder.

Jax nodded, wiping soggy cereal off his chin. "Fine." The clock on the stove read 7:33 AM. Who could be watching his video *now*?

"Dad," he asked, "did your parents ever video themselves?"

Mr. Opus shook his head. "I'm not sure, but I doubt it. They were pretty elderly by the time home video came along."

"Yeah, but is it possible they used it to . . . hypnotize people?"

Mr. Opus was horrified. "That works?"

Jax backed off. It was bad enough that his dad was afraid to look his own son in the face. The last thing he wanted was for his poor father to suspect every newscaster and talking head on TV.

It happened again during a social studies test in third period. There were Jax's eyes, where his essay answer on West Virginia coal exploration was supposed to be. He waited for the vision to dissipate, but instead of fading out, it grew stronger, until he could clearly see his irises darkening from royal blue to indigo. This was no fleeting impression. This kind of PIP image only came during a serious and sustained mesmeric link. When was it going to stop?

"Dude," Tommy whispered from the next seat, "you look like you need to change your underwear."

So Jax's distress was obvious to others as well. Only he didn't feel particularly distressed. Annoyed, maybe. Concerned. And . . . jealous?

Yes! Envy, the kind that kept you up nights and ate at your stomach lining. But who was he jealous of? Tommy? The other students who were able to write their test without interference?

All at once, he knew. This wasn't *his* envy. This emotion was coming through to him via the mesmeric link! The jealousy belonged to the person watching the video.

If there had been any doubt in Jax's mind that his clip was bending people, this blew it all away. And now it seemed that these remote hypnotisms could be every bit as powerful as the face-to-face kind.

At lunch, he called Sentia, but Dr. Mako was still unavailable.

"How many people are watching that clip I recorded?" he demanded of Ms. Samuels. "It can't just be at the institute. I got blowback while I was eating breakfast at seven thirty!"

"Let's not jump to conclusions until you've had a chance to speak to Dr. Mako," the assistant director suggested.

"And when's that going to be?" Jax complained bitterly. "I just experienced a link as strong as anything I've ever felt at the institute."

But Dr. Mako was not at Sentia that day or all that week. The visions continued, the PIP images becoming so clearly defined that Jax could make out the pores in his own skin. He was bombarded with emotions that had him jumping for joy one minute, and close to tears the next. In math one day, he picked up a fit of giggles so uncontrollable that he was sent to explain himself to the principal.

"What exactly was so funny?" Mr. Orenstein demanded.

"I honestly don't know," Jax replied. It might have been the first time in the history of school that this stock answer was 100 percent true.

It was as he left the office, stepping carefully, his eyesight still impaired, that the cause of his laughter came to him. He didn't *see* it — the PIP before him was still his own two eyes. Yet he *knew* it, the way you can conjure an image in your imagination. It was Singh One, stepping into a crowded room dressed from head to toe in a fluffy white bunny suit. Nothing had ever been more hilarious.

Correction, thought Jax. *Nothing has ever been more hilarious to the person thinking this.*

This was a mesmeric link with Singh Two! But why was he watching Jax's video?

By now, the visions had become so frequent that Jax no longer bothered to report them to Ms. Samuels. He picked up the flavor of intense competitiveness along with an image of a tennis court that might have come from Grace. But he didn't dare confront her. Until Dr. Mako made an official announcement that the threshold of remote hypnotism had been crossed, he had to keep a lid on this.

On Saturday, he arrived at Sentia to the news that Dr. Mako was not there and, no, he wasn't expected any time that day.

For Jax, it was the straw that broke the camel's back. His frustration reminded him of his very first week here, filling out endless tests while no one would even tell him what the institute was about. Only when he'd threatened to quit had Dr. Mako suddenly found an opening in his schedule for the Opus family.

Okay, maybe he had to try something similar now.

"I'm going home," he told Ms. Samuels. "Call me when Dr. Mako is ready to discuss what's been happening to me."

“Jax, this is really not being a team player,” the assistant director warned.

Jax tried to explain himself. “Nothing I could learn here today is half as important as what I have to tell Dr. Mako. Even if I stayed, I’d be useless to you.”

The elevator closed in front of him.

He was on the subway, hurtling downtown, when another vision hit abruptly. The picture was the same — the close-up of his eyes had become as familiar as the network logo in the corner of a TV monitor. But the emotion that came with it was brand-new and shocking in its intensity.

Hatred.

Jax held on to the pole he’d been leaning against. *The clip’s short,* he told himself. *It’ll pass.*

The PIP solidified into high definition, cutting off his view of his real surroundings. The strength of it — and its speed in revving up to full power — told him that this was going to be the most intense wave of blowback yet.

He didn’t hear the word. It was more like it appeared in his mind.

Dopus.

He should have known. Who else hated Jax this much? Who else was capable of so much pure corrosive acid?

Wilson.

The impressions followed in a parade, a slide show of intimidation.

“. . . at the corner of Forty-Fifth and Third . . . two AM . . .”

Wilson's voice.

"We'll meet at the corner of Forty-Fifth and Third . . ."

Jax's mind reeled. Wilson couldn't be planning a rendezvous while watching the video. So why were these words bubbling out of his thoughts? Jax sensed urgency and excitement, mixed with a touch of fear. Whatever this was, to Wilson, it was daring and super-important.

". . . two AM tonight . . . Get this right and everyone can forget all about Jackson Opus. . . ."

"Me?" Jax blurted aloud.

The vision dissipated, leaving him the object of curious stares from his fellow passengers. He glanced quickly away, only to notice that the train was pulling in to the Borough Hall station. He was in Brooklyn. Not only had he missed his stop, but also several others and a long tunnel into the next borough.

Wilson's words came back to him: *Get this right and everyone can forget all about Jackson Opus.*

What was that supposed to mean? A plan, obviously. Some sort of conspiracy to hurt Jax. But what? At two in the morning, he would be fast asleep in a doorman building with his parents in the next room. How could he be in danger?

Had Wilson figured out a way to reach him hypnotically? Through the blowback, maybe? Nobody was supposed to know about that. But Jax had been screaming it at Ms. Samuels for the better part of a week, so it wasn't inconceivable that the news had gotten out.

How was he vulnerable? He had no idea. None of this

was supposed to be possible in the first place, so logical reasoning could only take you so far. According to Dr. Mako, there was no such thing as remote hypnotism, which meant there should be no such thing as blowback. But that didn't change the fact that both were happening.

Gathering his wits and his book bag, Jax raced out the double doors and crossed over to the opposite platform to catch the next Manhattan-bound train home. His thoughts continued to whirl. How seriously should he take Wilson's words? Who had he been talking to? Jax had no way of knowing whether he'd "overheard" an actual conversation, or nothing more than the wishful thinking of a rotten jerk. Yet he was absolutely convinced that the threat was very real. There was something about Wilson's malevolence — the fierceness of his ill will — that told Jax this was no false alarm.

He had to find out.

But how?

20

Jax tiptoed through the darkened apartment, his sneakers in his hand, feet barely touching the floor. Mom and Dad were not light sleepers, but there was no explaining this little excursion, so he had to make sure they remained undisturbed.

The clock on the cable box read 1:12 AM as he let himself out the door, gingerly shutting and locking it behind him. He took the elevator not to the lobby, but to the basement laundry room. The building's front-desk staff wasn't usually nosy, but a twelve-year-old venturing out in the middle of the night would have raised an eyebrow or two.

He snaked through the gray cinderblock corridors, crawling on all fours past the entrance by the boiler room, where he knew there was a security camera. At the end of the hall was a heavy steel door leading to the alley. You couldn't get in that way, but you could slip out.

The streets were not deserted, but it was much quieter than in the daytime. Once on the avenue, Jax flitted three streets up and ducked down a block of apartments that had once been nineteenth-century tenements.

The buildings had been redone, but the old-fashioned fire escapes were still there, the wrought iron freshly repainted.

He stopped under the third house in and stood among the garbage cans, waiting. Soon, a low gonging sound told him someone was on the way down. The shadowy shape came into view, backlit by the streetlamp. The tall figure reached the end of stairway and whistled.

"I'm here," Jax called softly.

The ladder at the bottom of the fire escape could be lowered to street level, but that would bring about a screech of metal that would attract everyone for thirty blocks. Instead, the climber hung from the lowest rung, and Jax moved forward to catch him and ease him to the ground. At least, that's the way it should have gone in theory. In reality, the two went sprawling into a pile of garbage bags.

"Nice catch," Tommy growled.

Jax grinned and hauled his friend upright. "Good thing garbage day isn't till tomorrow."

"I already hate you, man, and this thing hasn't even started yet. Do you know what happens to me if my old man snores himself awake and checks my room?"

Jax was contrite. "Maybe I shouldn't have gotten you involved."

"Oh, sure," Tommy retorted. "Go out there and get yourself killed. It's always about you."

"It might be about nothing," Jax reminded him. "I didn't even hear it. It's more like I pulled it out of some guy's mind. It could have been a daydream, and none of it's real."

Tommy shrugged irritably. "I don't know what to hope for. If it's nothing, it isn't worth all the hassle. And if it's something, I'm definitely scared of it."

"We won't know until we get there," Jax pointed out. "Come on. You miss a train at this hour, you've got a long wait for the next one."

The two rode the subway to Forty-Second Street and walked to the corner of Forty-Fifth and Third. They ducked into the recessed doorway of a closed locksmith's shop and surveyed the intersection. It was quieter here than it had been downtown. The multitudes who worked in this neighborhood rarely stuck around so late. Office buildings, banks, stores, restaurants — all closed except for a twenty-four-hour Japanese noodle shop, which had no customers at the moment.

"Maybe your ESP radar picked up some guy's takeout order," Tommy whispered.

"Shhhh!" Jax felt a rush of chagrin. Hypnotism was unscientific enough the way Dr. Mako practiced it — with an entire institute studying it like they were splitting the atom. For a newbie like Jax to run off half-cocked over every random burp of his brain was pretty flaky. And to get poor Tommy mixed up in it . . .

"Incoming," Tommy intoned.

It was Wilson, approaching along Third Avenue. He wore black jeans and a black jacket, his collar upturned, the brim of his Yankees baseball cap pulled low. But nothing could disguise the arrogance in his posture.

I wasn't wrong, Jax thought to himself. Something was going down.

They melted farther into the doorway as Wilson passed by. Tommy mouthed the words *Big dude.*

Jax nodded. "Big ego, small brain," he murmured back.

Another black-clad figure crossed the street and joined Wilson. Jax recognized him instantly.

"DeRon," he whispered to Tommy. "Wilson's sidekick. A little less muscle — everywhere except his head."

"Now can we go home?" Tommy asked hopefully.

"Not till we find out what they're up to."

Wilson and DeRon exchanged a few words and then headed west on Forty-Fifth. Jax watched them disappear, raising a hand to keep Tommy from running after them. They didn't want to lose the two hypnos, but they couldn't risk being spotted either. After a breathless thirty seconds, they scampered around the corner and took cover behind a mailbox.

Wilson and DeRon were about a third of the way down the long block, at the door of a lit storefront. Apparently, the noodle shop wasn't the only establishment in the neighborhood open at this hour.

Jax and Tommy crossed to the other side and approached at a jog, keeping low in the shelter of parked cars. There stood Wilson, DeRon at his side, in what looked like conversation with a uniformed night watchman on the inside. After a moment, the guard slipped a latch and held the door wide open.

"He knows them," Tommy observed. "I thought they were going to break in or torch the place or something."

Jax shook his head. "He doesn't know them. Wilson bent him. Right through the glass."

"Whoa." Tommy was impressed. "Could you do that to get us into a Knicks game?"

"Concentrate." Jax watched as the two hypnos looked around the store. He couldn't imagine what kind of business it might be. The lighting was dim, but bright enough to show that every inch of the floor was taken up with desks. Filing cabinets rose to the ceiling. The only empty wall space was plastered with posters. Jax squinted.

Governor Zachary Schaumberg

for President

VOTE SCHAUMBERG

★ ★ ★ IN THE ★ ★ ★

DEMOCRATIC PRIMARY

we back zach.

"Schaumberg," Tommy commented. "Isn't that the guy from North Carolina running for president? What do a couple of teenage hypnotists care about him?"

It came to Jax in a wave of revelation. "This guy's running against Trey Douglas for the Democratic nomination! Trey Douglas is a major supporter of Sentia."

"Yeah, but what does this have to do with you?" Tommy wondered. "How can something that happens in a campaign office in the middle of the night mean that everybody can forget about *you*?"

Wilson pulled two large canvas laundry bags out of a backpack. Jax and Tommy watched as the two hypnos began opening file drawers and dumping the contents into their sacks. While this was going on, the guard sat at his post, playing solitaire on a computer screen.

"Remind me never to hire that guy to guard anything I care about," Tommy commented.

"That's not it," Jax insisted. "He's bent. He probably thinks he's alone and the office is secure. Or maybe he's been hypnotized to believe they're the cleaning crew picking up trash."

"Could you un-hypnotize him?" Tommy suggested. "Get him to see what's going on right under his nose?"

Jax shook his head. "Too risky. Wilson and DeRon can get ugly. I don't want that poor guy to end up in the hospital because of us."

"Yeah, but you've got to look after yourself, man," Tommy insisted. "What if their plan is to wreck the place and get it blamed on you? Maybe they've got something of yours to leave on the floor to frame you. Or they hypnotized the guard to say you did it."

"Or maybe it's got nothing to do with me," Jax countered. "They must think there's something in those files that can help Trey Douglas win the election."

"But how does that add up to 'everyone can forget about Jackson Opus'?"

"They'll be heroes," Jax reasoned. "And Dr. Mako will stop concentrating on me, and will focus on them and what they can do for Sentia."

"Why don't we call the cops?" Tommy suggested.

Jax thought it over. He wasn't too fond of Wilson and DeRon, but getting them arrested could mean trouble for Dr. Mako and Sentia. Jax resented the way the director had been stringing him along lately, but he couldn't risk the institute being shut down. It was the only organization that took hypnotism seriously — except for Axel Braintree's collection of losers.

"We do nothing right now," he decided. "I'm a witness and you're my backup. If it ever comes to that, we'll tell."

Their bags full to bursting, Wilson and DeRon headed back to the security guard. Wilson spoke to the man, who then got up and went to sit in an open empty file drawer, his legs stuffed uncomfortably in front of him. As a finishing touch, Wilson ordered him to suck his thumb. Laughing uproariously, the two exited the storefront and disappeared down the block, hunched under their burdens.

"What a jerk!" Tommy hissed. "Come on, the least we can do is get that poor guy out of the file cabinet."

Jax shook his head. "He's a security guard. He could be armed."

Tommy was confused. "If he's got a gun, why didn't he pull it on the two idiots who stuck him in the drawer?"

"You saw how it went down. He was hypnotized from the start."

"So? *Re*-hypnotize him."

"It's too risky," Jax explained. "If you bend a subject who's already bent, there's a chance that commands from the different hypnos will contradict each other. Like if I tell him to remember after Wilson's told him to forget, he might try to do both. That kind of struggle could turn his mind into mush. People have been driven crazy that way — we learned about it in History of Hypnotism."

Tommy looked haunted. "You know, I was kind of jealous of you because you could bamboozle people into giving you free hamburgers and stuff. But this creeps me out. I mean, the file cabinet's bad enough. But they could have made him do anything — jump off a building or stick his head in the furnace or chug-a-lug Drano. It's too much power."

Jax nodded in agreement. "That's why you need an outfit like Sentia to study it and make sure it's used for good instead of . . . well, you see for yourself what it can be used for."

Jax heard the words as they passed his lips and wondered if he even believed them anymore.

21

Principal Orenstein was a cadaverous man with perpetually smeared glasses, so he always seemed to be peering through a fog. "Well," he said, squinting at the scorch marks on Jax's sleeve. "I suppose there's no permanent damage."

Jax had the grace to look abashed. In the science lab, he'd been struck by more blowback. The vision had been so intense he hadn't noticed that his shirtsleeve had caught fire from his Bunsen burner. If it hadn't been for Tommy shaking a bottle of orange soda and shooting a spray like an extinguisher, Jax might have suffered serious burns.

It had been going on all weekend, too. Yesterday, in the plush waiting room of Dad's Bentley dealership, a PIP image had caught him unawares, and he'd keeled over into the arms of a rapper who'd been there spending the proceeds of his last platinum album. The scariest part was that the visions were definitely getting stronger. If they could make him lose his balance or set his clothes on fire, what was next? Would he wander off the sidewalk in front of a speeding taxi?

"What concerns me isn't so much the accident itself," the principal went on, "but when Mr. Morrison tried to help you, you pushed him away and told him to mind his own business. What happens in his classroom *is* his business."

There was no explaining this one. "Sorry." He gazed into Mr. Orenstein's eyes to make sure the principal understood he was sincere.

"I'm afraid we've gone beyond the level of a mere apology, Jackson. You laid hands on a teacher. According to the school's code of conduct . . ."

With that, the principal seemed to lose his train of thought. A PIP image bubbled up in front of Jax.

He hypnotized himself looking at me!

"Yes, well," the principal murmured drowsily, his eyes still locked on Jax's, "you're a good kid — one of our best, really. I think we can give you another chance."

"That would be great —" And suddenly, Jax's relief morphed into anger. At that moment, he understood his father's total rejection of his family background. In a way, Jax felt it even more acutely. Dad had to deal with hypnotists, but at least he'd never been saddled with the "gift" itself. Just then, Jax wished he'd never heard of the Opuses or the Sparkses or Sentia or the wondrous Elias Mako. He longed for the days when he thought *bent* meant *crooked*.

"What do you mean 'another chance'?" he blurted. "I pushed a teacher! That's as bad as punching him in the face! You can't let me get away with that! You've got to throw the book at me. . . ." He wasn't sure what he was trying to accomplish. Getting in trouble at school wasn't going to un-complicate his life. But he rejected any special treatment courtesy of this unwanted skill he'd inherited.

"Agreed," Mr. Orenstein exclaimed. "I'm suspending you for two weeks. And when you come back, I want to see you and your parents in this office."

At the mention of Mom and Dad, Jax's will to be punished evaporated. "Maybe the second chance is a better way to go."

"My thoughts exactly," the principal concurred.

Jax concentrated on his sneakers to break the link.

"I'm glad that's settled," Mr. Orenstein went on. "I hate to see any problem with one of our best and brightest. Tell me, how are you getting along at Dr. Mako's institute? What was the name?"

"Sentia," Jax supplied. "To be honest, it hasn't really turned out like I expected. I don't think I'm going to go anymore."

The principal did not approve. "You can't rob yourself of the opportunity to work with a man like Dr. Mako!"

"Actually, he's kind of a disappointment, too." It was the first time Jax had admitted such a thing out loud.

Mr. Orenstein was appalled. "Dr. Elias Mako has devoted his life to New York City education and is an inspiration to every single one of us!"

Jax labored to keep the sarcasm out of his tone. "Yeah, so I've been told."

"Dr. Mako's circle of associates reads like a Who's Who. Why, one of the institute's best friends is Senator Douglas, and now it looks like he may have the Democratic nomination wrapped up. Especially after the scandal about Governor Schaumberg."

Jax froze. "Governor Schaumberg?"

The principal made a face. "It's all the usual political skulduggery. It happens so often these days that it's hardly worth thinking about. What's important about this is that it's a couple of weeks before the primary, and it'll probably sink Schaumberg and put Douglas over the top. A lucky piece of timing for the senator."

Jax had a mental picture of Wilson and DeRon scurrying down Forty-Fifth Street carrying Schaumberg's stolen files in canvas sacks. *Lucky timing?*

Luck probably had very little to do with it.

Jax went straight from the office to the library, pouncing on a computer to get the latest news. It was true. The governor had issued a permit for a casino in North Carolina in exchange for a large campaign contribution. Schaumberg claimed he knew nothing about it. But even if that was true, the damage was already done. The story was all over the Internet. CNN and Fox were both screaming about it on their live feeds. The papers were planning major headlines. Even if Governor Schaumberg turned out to be innocent, there was no way his name would be cleared by primary day.

Jax couldn't believe it. Wilson DeVries was a bully and a mean-spirited, obnoxious idiot. But Jax had always assumed that he couldn't do much damage beyond the range of the handful of unfortunates who got in his way.

Not anymore.

Before he knew it, Jax was out of the building and

running for the subway, classes forgotten — not that he could have concentrated on school if he'd happened to be there. At the newsstand on the platform, he bought a *New York Post.* The front page blazoned *SHAME ON SCHAUMBERG* in capital letters three inches high.

"It's good to see you, Jax," Ms. Samuels told him when he got to Sentia. "Dr. Mako and I felt terrible about the way you left on Saturday."

In answer, Jax slammed the *Post* on her desk.

"Yes, I heard," she told him. "An awful story, but it's a real break for Senator Douglas's campaign —"

"Wilson and DeRon did this!" Jax interrupted savagely.

"I'm not following you."

"I *saw* those two guys break into Schaumberg's headquarters and steal the files! Now suddenly this big scandal comes out! No way that's a coincidence!"

She looked so utterly blindsided that Jax softened his tone. He explained how he'd picked up Wilson's plan through hypnotic blowback, and had staked out the rendezvous point to see what was going on.

Ms. Samuels was still bewildered. "But why would Wilson and DeRon do such a thing?"

"Don't you see? They did it to make points with Dr. Mako because he supports Douglas. Wilson's exact words were 'Get this right and everyone can forget all about Jackson Opus.' They did it to turn the spotlight off me and onto them!"

"This is a very serious accusation!" the assistant director exclaimed. "I have to talk to Dr. Mako."

"Yeah, well, I hope you have better luck than me," Jax muttered.

"Please wait in the lounge. Dr. Mako will be here within the hour."

Jax had intended to make a dramatic exit, but the prospect of finally seeing the director changed his mind. Regardless of this sleazy business of Wilson and DeRon and Governor Schaumberg, there was still the issue of Jax's video and the ongoing bouts of blowback. Only Dr. Mako could advise him what to do about that.

In the lounge, Jax helped himself to a granola bar and sat down at one of the computers to read up on the Schaumberg scandal. The headlines were spiraling out of control: *SCHAUMBERG SCHMEAR* and *KASINO KICKBACK KO'S KANDIDATE*. Strangely, there was no story at all about a burglary at Schaumberg's headquarters, or even passing mention of a night watchman stuffed in a file drawer. It was possible that the governor and his people were trying to let the story fade. The mystery of a security guard with no recollection of a massive break-in would only give the scandal a longer life.

The door of the lounge was flung open, and Wilson burst into the room with his customary brashness. He seemed surprised to see Jax at the computer. "How come you're so early, Dopus?"

Jax glared back. "How come *you* are?"

Wilson brayed a laugh. "I couldn't sit still at school. This is a big day. A humongous day."

"Oh, I know."

Wilson's eyes narrowed. "What do you know?"

"I saw you, Saturday night, you and DeRon. I know exactly what you did and how you did it."

"You're lying." Wilson snorted. But he looked a little less sure of himself.

"I know you guys broke into Schaumberg headquarters. I saw you bend that poor guard and steal those files. And give me the credit to put two and two together and figure out where this big election scandal comes from."

"You little . . ." Wilson stormed over to Jax and stood too close. "Have you been spying on me? How could you possibly know where we were going to be Saturday night?"

Jax could feel the violence emanating from his enemy like heat from a furnace, but he did not flinch. "How long have you been at this place, Wilson? Haven't you noticed that people here can do things? Maybe I've got something going on that you don't have a prayer of understanding. And no matter what you do for Trey Douglas's campaign, it's not going to make you a better mind-bender than me."

Wilson reached out with a meaty hand, but Jax wheeled his chair out of the way just in time. He jumped up and faced the bully, jaw set. "You asked what I'm doing here so early. I'm here to rat you out. Let's see what Dr. Mako thinks of the way you and your scumball friend operate."

Jax thought Wilson was going to come after him again. Instead, the big boy threw his head back and laughed. "Dopus, every time I think I'm going to have to beat your face in, you prove that you're too dumb to be a threat. You want to tell on me to Mako? Be my guest. Who do you think sent us out there to get those files?"

"You're lying!" Jax roared in a fury.

"Think about it, genius," Wilson tossed over his shoulder, and he left the lounge.

Jax was stricken with shock. Could it be true that Dr. Mako was the mastermind behind all this? To burglarize a campaign office — and to use hypnotism to do it — went against everything Elias Mako stood for.

Or at least everything he *said* he stood for.

Of course, that depended on Wilson telling the truth, which wasn't exactly a slam dunk. But come to think of it, Wilson wasn't the first person to suggest that Elias Mako wasn't as pure as his public image. What about Axel Braintree, the head of the Sandman's Guild? He had tried to recruit Jax to be his spy because he didn't trust Mako. At the time, Jax had dismissed it as paranoia. And it *was* paranoid. For example, if the director was dirty, why would a respected presidential hopeful like Trey Douglas go along with his scheming? And yet Douglas was Dr. Mako's close friend and greatest admirer. Jax and his parents had heard it from the man's own lips: *You're a lucky young man to have Dr. Mako in your corner. He's devoted his life to New York City education and is an inspiration to every single one of us.*

That sentence had pulled him up short before, but this time he very nearly choked on it. As if in a daze, he rolled his chair back to the computer and opened up YouTube. One by one, he searched the keywords *Elias Mako* along with the names of the director's many famous acquaintances. The video clips told the whole shocking story. Without exception, each celebrity used virtually the same words to describe the director of the Sentia institute: *Dr. Elias Mako has devoted his life to New York City education and is an inspiration to every single one of us.*

No wonder the director had so many powerful supporters. They weren't flocking to his banner. He was hypnotizing them!

And if Trey Douglas won the nomination and then went on to win the White House, Mako would control the leader of the free world.

Jax was still reeling from this revelation when the door swung wide and none other than Dr. Mako himself stood before him. It would be wrong to say he looked disheveled, but his very expensive suit was slightly rumpled, and his perfect Windsor knot was uncharacteristically off center.

"I came as soon as I heard." He wasn't out of breath exactly, but it was clear that he'd made great haste to get there.

For more than a week, Jax had begged for an audience with this man. His every thought had been to reach the director so they could discuss the undeniable truth that remote hypnotism was possible and that his video was accomplishing it. But now, face-to-face with him, all he could come up with was: "I don't have anything to say to you."

It was the first time Jax had ever seen Mako in a state

of less-than-complete comfort and control. "Jackson, the only reason I support Trey Douglas is because he would make a fine president. Having a friend of Sentia in the Oval Office would be good for all of us."

"That means nothing to me," Jax replied evenly, "because I'm not a part of Sentia anymore. I'm out of here."

He walked out of the room, down the stairs instead of using the elevator, and through the lobby into the fresh air.

It had never tasted fresher.

22

"Anyway, the good news is you've got your life back," Tommy commented philosophically.

A bike messenger hurtled by, passing so close on the narrow Brooklyn Bridge pedestrian path that the man's flapping windbreaker stung Jax's shoulder.

"Really?" Tommy shouted at the rapidly receding cyclist.

It was the kind of near miss that happened every minute in New York. But lately, Jax had been so wrapped up in Sentia that he'd taken himself out of the bump and grind of living in a city of more than eight million people. A big fringe benefit of quitting Dr. Mako was that his time was his own once again. A walk across the bridge would have been out of the question on a Sentia day.

"Well, I finish my homework before midnight now, so that's a plus," Jax admitted. "But I'm still getting blowback from that video I did. I don't know what Mako's thinking, but I hope he gets a new hobby real soon."

"Maybe he has dinner parties and you're the entertainment," Tommy joked. "'Get a load of the guy with the multicolored eyes. They're blue; they're green; they're purple with pink polka dots. . . .'"

Jax was no longer listening. Over the noises of the intermittent traffic, he could hear the sound of someone in terrible distress, sobbing as if the end of the world were at hand. Then, perhaps a hundred feet ahead, he caught sight of a dark-clad figure darting across the three Manhattan-bound lanes to the rail at the edge of the bridge.

Tommy saw it, too. "What's that guy doing?"

They watched in horror as the young man hoisted himself over the barrier and stood poised, trembling, on the narrow ledge.

A cry was torn from Jax's throat. "Don't do it, mister! Come back!"

Jax and Tommy leaped the divider and dodged across the lanes, ignoring the squeal of brakes and the chorus of angry car horns.

"Don't jump!" Jax shouted.

"You don't want to do that!" Tommy added urgently.

They reached the opposite side and approached the jumper, hugging the rail.

"Don't come any closer!" the man warned.

Jax halted. "Okay! Okay! But let's talk about this!"

"There's nothing to talk about," the man groaned in despair. "I have no choice!"

Cars continued to whiz by, horns blaring, passing dangerously close to Jax and Tommy. No one seemed to notice that there was a man just a few feet away about to end his own life.

Jax tried to be as soothing as possible. "There's always

a choice, and there's always hope! I know it!" But even as he said the words, he realized that he was not up to this task. How could he convince such a despondent soul that life was worth living? He wasn't a psychologist. He wasn't even an adult! How could he talk this person into choosing life over death?

The jumper looked down at the swirling waters of the East River far below and set his jaw with determination.

"No!!" Jax howled.

The man shot him a frantic glance, and Jax understood exactly what he had to do. He held the gaze, pouring on every ounce of mesmeric concentration he'd ever learned from the likes of Elias Mako. He wasn't at all sure it was possible to get through to someone in this state of desperation. When the faint PIP image appeared, he thought at first that it might be more blowback from the video. But no — it was himself on the bridge, Tommy over his shoulder, cars passing far too close behind them.

It's working! I can do this!

Classic hypnotic technique usually started by instructing the subject to relax, but that wasn't such a good idea with a man on a ledge. If he got too relaxed, he might fall. "Okay, mister, everything's going to be fine. Your mind is calm, but your grip on the rail is very firm. That's the most important thing now — hanging on to the rail."

The man's knuckles whitened on the bar. So far, so good. Tommy looked on, pale and wide-eyed.

"Now listen carefully. You *want* to be on *this* side of

the barrier. It's all that's ever mattered to you in the world. So climb over and stand right beside me."

Obediently, the jumper swung a leg over the rail and paused uncertainly. Jax was aware of the PIP image swinging away from himself and Tommy, where it faded, stabilized, and then winked out altogether.

I've lost him! he thought frantically.

The man shivered for a moment, as if waking from a dream. Then he began to teeter backward toward the edge.

With a cry of shock, Jax reached out and took hold of the man's arm. "Grab him!" he shouted to Tommy.

His friend seized the other arm and held on for dear life. "What happened?" he babbled. "I thought you hypnotized him to climb back!"

"He got away from me!" Jax panted. "He's so stressed out that the connection failed as soon as he broke eye contact! Come on, let's pull him over!"

They pulled with all their might, but the jumper was a deadweight, and they couldn't budge him.

"What are we going to do?" asked Tommy, wild with fear.

"I'll have to bend him again," Jax decided.

"Because it worked so great last time?"

Jax struggled to explain. "I'm going to give him a posthypnotic suggestion. Then I'll wake him up, and give the trigger word for him to climb back on his own."

Distraught and confused, the man was harder to mesmerize this time. But soon the PIP image was firmly in place, and Jax implanted his suggestion. "I'm going to bring you back in a minute with the snap of my fingers, and you will feel happy and relaxed — but not too relaxed. And when you hear the word *pickles*, you'll climb the rest of the way over and stand beside me. You'll remember nothing of all this except that your life is precious to you."

It took Jax every ounce of courage he had to still his shaking hand so he could snap his fingers. Straddling the rail, the man came to himself with a start, his entire body stiffening.

"What —?"

"Pickles!" Jax exclaimed swiftly.

The response was immediate. The jumper swung his left leg over the barrier and was a jumper no more. Jax and Tommy hustled him across the three lanes of traffic to the pedestrian walkway.

Jax looked at his subject anxiously. "How do you feel?"

The man was furious. "You've got some nerve asking me that! You're the idiot who dragged me through three lanes of traffic. You could have gotten me killed. Don't you know life is precious? Moron!" And he ran off, still muttering angrily to himself.

Tommy faced his friend. "Pickles?"

Jax shrugged. "There wasn't time to get creative. And I figured, who talks about pickles on a bridge? Anyway, it worked."

Tommy whistled with admiration. "It sure did. You saved that guy's life. Maybe you should go back to the institute after all."

Jax stopped in his tracks. "You're kidding, right? After what I've told you about Dr. Mako?"

"Well, you've got to admit you never could have pulled this off without all that stuff he taught you," Tommy reasoned.

"I don't care if he taught me how to perform photosynthesis. He's hypnotized half the US Congress and most of the Fortune 500. And if he gets his way, our next president will be nothing but a puppet, on a string held by the great Elias Mako. I'm never going near that guy again! He's poison."

Tommy blinked. "Dr. Elias Mako has devoted his life to New York City education and is an inspiration to every single one of us."

Jax was appalled. "What did you just say?"

Tommy repeated it, word for word. And as he did, it was like we wasn't Tommy anymore. He was a drone, no longer in control of his thoughts.

Jax stared at his friend. "He got to you!"

"Who?" Tommy was mystified. "You mean Mako? I've never even met him!"

"You just said the exact same sentence as everybody he bends into loving him!"

"Don't you think I'd know if some Dr. Frankenstein knocked on my door and put me under?" Tommy demanded.

Jax waved in the direction where the former jumper had stormed off. "That guy — does he know he almost jumped off a bridge and I hypnotized him? Twice?"

"No, not until some waiter asks if he wants pickles and he climbs on top of the salad bar." Tommy looked suddenly troubled. "So you think Mako bent me and made me forget about it? But why? I'm nobody."

"You're my best friend. It was a message — he can get to me through the people who are closest to me. I'll bet that whole business with the jumper was a setup! And he hypnotized you to remind me how much I need him and Sentia."

Tommy looked astonished. "No chance! What would have happened if we hadn't run over to save the guy?"

Jax shrugged. "That's the kind of quality person who might have a hammerlock on the next president of the United States."

A deep sense of dread took hold in Jax's stomach and began to rise up his esophagus. He'd thought he was through with Sentia, free and clear. But obviously, Mako wasn't finished with him yet.

The director still wanted something from Jackson Opus.

The pictures that decorated the outer office seemed different now. Jax no longer saw the crème de la crème of global influence and fame. He looked at the photographs for what they were: a trophy wall. Dr. Mako, the smiling hunter, his boot resting on the big game he'd bagged — celebs, CEOs, and politicians, instead of elephants and rhinos. And, possibly, one future president.

It's none of your business, a voice inside Jax's head said very clearly. *What are you even doing here? You quit this place!*

Tommy's words came back to him, twisting in his gut: *Dr. Elias Mako has devoted his life . . .*

The fact that the director had hypnotized Tommy said more about his ruthlessness than anything else he had done. It was a statement that meant you couldn't quit Mako — not unless Mako was willing to let you go.

But I'm not going to get pushed around.

Ms. Samuels seemed uneasy as she escorted him into the office. Nervousness suited her, as did everything else.

And then Jax was face-to-face with the man himself. Mako rose, perhaps not so much in welcome as to display his height advantage and physical superiority. Oddly, when Jax peered into the dark eyes under those heavy brows, he was aware of an inexplicable impulse to impress this important, powerful man. It made no sense. Mako was the enemy, and Jax knew it. Yet the feeling persisted.

"I apologize that my schedule has been so heavy lately," the director began as the two seated themselves. "Ms. Samuels mentioned that you wanted to meet. And I had a feeling that certain events might have you jump to the conclusion that you needed to talk to me."

The way Dr. Mako said *jump* jarred Jax back to himself, and he lashed out in anger. "You put that jumper on the Brooklyn Bridge yesterday!"

Dr. Mako shifted his long frame in his chair and looked interested. "If there was a jumper," he said carefully, "I'm confident that we have developed your abilities to the point where your hypnotic skill would enable you to save a life."

"And if I'd been tying my shoelaces while the guy ran over to the rail?"

The director smiled thinly. "No scientist can eliminate every variable from an experiment."

"Was my friend Tommy an experiment, too? Or was he just a message?"

Dr. Mako looked impatient. "Surely this isn't why you've been clamoring to see me all this time."

"It isn't," Jax agreed. "The recording — the one you said couldn't hypnotize people. It's hypnotizing people, isn't it?"

"Well, there you caught me in a little fib," the director admitted. "It was the truth that remote mesmerism had never been accomplished. But I believed — I *hoped* — that your remarkable gift would change that. I've shown your clip to dozens of subjects, with impressive results."

"Yeah —" Jax was bitter. "I've been getting the blowback to prove it. I'm almost nuts — not to mention that I nearly got kicked out of school."

"For that I apologize," Dr. Mako said formally. "Of course, I suspected that some form of the mesmeric link would be created, but I couldn't be sure."

"Yeah, you could've," Jax retorted, "if you'd bothered to answer any of my five thousand calls."

"We may disagree on method," the director conceded, "but surely you see the importance of this breakthrough. You're a part of mesmeric history, just like the Opuses of the past."

"And the Sparkses?" Jax prompted.

The surprise on Mako's face was worth it. He even stammered a little when he said, "I — I wasn't certain that you were aware of your mother's family. They haven't been active in many generations."

"You keep a lot of secrets. Like how Wilson and DeRon stole Governor Schaumberg's files. Or the way you make all your famous friends — by bending them."

The director was clearly caught off guard, but when he spoke again, it was in the ringing tone of a preacher giving a sermon. "The story of civilization is filled with tales of people who changed the world because they were willing to use whatever means at their disposal to achieve their goals. Our turn has come, and the means we use will be our gift. *Your* gift."

"How can a guy like me change the world?" Jax challenged. "I can't even whistle."

"Not only are you in a position to change the world, but you're the only one who can. You alone have the ability to hypnotize remotely. You will record another clip — it will be released over the Internet via a computer virus that will self-erase as soon as it's been viewed. In it, you will implant a post-hypnotic suggestion for the viewer to vote for Senator Douglas in the New York primary. If he wins New York, the nomination is a mathematical certainty."

Horror flooded every inch of Jax's being. Even though he had guessed at Mako's intention to put Trey Douglas in the White House, the diabolical nature of this plan was shattering.

"That's the worst thing I've ever heard in my life!" Jax gasped. "If it isn't illegal, that's only because no one could imagine such a sleazy, terrible, evil thing. Elections are supposed to be honest and free! To steal one by reaching into people's minds and telling them who to vote for — that goes against everything America is supposed to be about."

The director was unapologetic. "Sometimes, Jackson, true greatness can only be achieved through extraordinary methods."

"You mean by cheating," Jax accused.

"That word falls far short of describing a revolution in which every aspect of how things are accomplished is turned on its ear."

Jax folded his arms in front of him. "There's only one problem. You can't do it without me, and I say no."

Dr. Mako didn't flinch. "I'm asking you to reconsider."

"I'd rather throw *myself* off that bridge."

"Interesting," the director told him. "You know what else is interesting? How quickly you deduced that I'd paid a visit to your little friend Tommy. Yet it never occurred to you to wonder who else I might have dropped in on."

Jax jerked forward. "Like who?"

"Dear old Mom and Dad. Your father is a fascinating case study. Excellent taste in fine automobiles, but very conflicted when it comes to his son's talents. Of course, it can't be easy to be an Opus with no hypnotic ability —"

"What did you do to them?" Jax fairly shouted.

"I made a little suggestion. I won't bore you with the details, but rest assured they are in absolutely no danger as long as you are cooperative. If not, suffice it to say you will find yourself an orphan very quickly."

In a frenzy of terror mixed with rage, Jax leaned forward and fixed his former mentor with the most powerful gaze he could manage. Dr. Mako's eyes registered shock for an instant, then went blank as the PIP image began to materialize between them.

I've got him! Jax thought triumphantly, racking his brain for the perfect mesmeric message to implant in this evil mind. This was his chance not just to protect Mom and Dad, but to make sure Elias Mako could never hurt or control anybody again. But how to do it? Could a hypnotic suggestion cripple someone else's power? Or perhaps he could bend the director into forgetting his own mesmeric abilities. Unfortunately, the best person to ask would be Mako himself, which was obviously not an option. . . .

The hesitation cost him dearly. For a moment, he was aware of the stirring sensation, as if his subject was trying to hypnotize him back. And an instant later he was struck with a mental blast that felt like a three-hour headache compressed into a single surge of brain freeze. The PIP vanished, obliterating the link. The force of it threw Jax back in his chair, whacking his head against the wall. Chagrined, he at least had the satisfaction of seeing that Mako was equally shaken.

The director's discomfiture did not last long. He uttered a cold laugh. "The power may be stronger in you, but I still have a few tricks up my sleeve. I advise you not to try that again. For your sake — and your parents'."

Jax knew he'd been outmaneuvered by an expert, and that he had no choice but to give in. "If I do this for you," he said, panting, defeated, "how do I know you won't trigger the suggestion anyway?"

"Jackson, you have my word."

Jax stared in dismay. Did Elias Mako honestly believe his word was worth any more than the breath it took to blow it out his mouth?

Lab 3 had been converted into a TV studio, complete with state-of-the-art lighting and foam soundproof tile on the walls. Ray Finklemeyer was not present this time; Dr. Mako controlled the recording by remote.

The director was taking no chances with the exact wording of his message. It was all on a teleprompter mounted on the camera itself.

"Look into my eyes . . ." Jax read from the prompter, his face tightly framed in the monitor. "Concentrate. . . . You are relaxed and happy. . . ."

"Again," Dr. Mako ordered. "I need more intensity this time. The virus will have you appearing on computer screens as a pop-up. You'll have perhaps two seconds to reach people before they delete the window. Act like this means something to you — because it does."

Jax gulped and started over. It was obvious that the director took this deadly seriously and wanted to get it exactly right.

". . . In a moment, I will disappear. You will remember nothing of me or this message. Life will continue as usual. But the next time you operate the lever of a voting booth, it will be your overwhelming desire to vote for Trey Douglas."

For nearly two hours, Dr. Mako and Jax worked on crafting the video clip until the director was satisfied he had what he needed.

"Thank you for all your time and effort," Dr. Mako said at last. As if he hadn't just threatened to kill Jax's family.

“When does the message go out?” Jax asked in trepidation.

“Our tech people have already created the virus that will carry it,” the director explained. “But we want to do more tests to make sure there’s no evidence of the video once it’s been viewed. A couple of days, perhaps.” He grinned. “You’ll know.”

It hit Jax like an electric shock. He had practically been flattened by the PIP images generated by a clip shown around Sentia a few dozen times. What would the blow-back be like from a viral video that was designed to reach hundreds of thousands, maybe even millions?

Dr. Mako read his thoughts. “It will be an interesting first few days. But you’ll learn to cope.”

“What about my parents?” Jax prodded. “You have to take out that suggestion!”

“In time, Jackson. In time.”

The first vision came in gym class during a volleyball game. It was faint but unmistakable — his own talking head in a pop-up on a computer screen. There was no sound, of course, but if he concentrated, he could almost read his own lips:

. . . vote for Trey Douglas . . .

Wham! The ball came screaming in at light speed, hitting him full in the face. The impact was so powerful that his nose was still bleeding in the nurse's office twenty minutes later.

Tommy spotted him a fresh T-shirt. "What happened, man? Why didn't you put your hand up?"

Jax hesitated. "It was blowback."

"Still?"

Jax shook his head. "Again. I made another clip."

"Why would you do a stupid thing like that?" Tommy demanded. "Especially after what happened last time?"

"I had no choice." He told Tommy about Dr. Mako's threat against the Opuses.

Tommy was round-eyed. "And you believe him?"

"I have to! Look at what he did to the guy on the

bridge. And he admitted that he bent you to get you to sing his praises and then wiped your memory of it."

"You said being color-blind makes me a tough nut," Tommy challenged, still not entirely convinced.

"Only to me. All hypnotists are different. No one really understands the science of why it works." He tossed his blood-soaked T-shirt in the garbage and pulled on Tommy's. "Think of the subjects at Sentia. The hypnos get them to run on treadmills, and jump up and down, and do a bunch of harmless stuff. But we could just as easily have them pushing each other off roofs or down stairs, or even shooting people in the head. From a mesmeric standpoint, there's no difference. It's just the details of what you tell them to do."

"This is really messed up," Tommy decided. "Maybe you should go to your folks. At least let them know they're in danger."

"That's the *worst* thing I could possibly do," Jax said despairingly. "They'd run to the cops, who couldn't help even if they believed the story. Best case scenario, the police would think we were wackos. Because if they take us seriously, they'll question Mako. Then he'll know I'm behind it, and he'll activate the suggestion that'll kill my parents."

Another jolt of blowback sent Jax reeling.

"Watch your nose, Opus," Tommy advised. "That's my last spare shirt."

Jax recovered enough to glare at him. "Your wardrobe problems are breaking my heart."

"Listen, man," Tommy said seriously. "I get that you think there's no way out of this. But if you somehow come up with a way to fight back, I'm in."

Jax was rattled by visions several times that day, including once in science, when he overturned a beaker of acid on his sneakers. Disturbingly, the incidents seemed to be coming closer together as the day wore on. He had a mental picture of the computer virus spreading — his face appearing on screen after screen, planting the suggestion inside unsuspecting voters. Worse than the blowback itself was the undeniable truth that he was tampering with a free and fair election — and possibly helping a ruthless person like Dr. Mako gain a scary amount of power.

He staggered through his schedule, the toe of his sock poking out of the hole in his shoe, his complexion pale, his forehead beaded with sweat. Several teachers asked if he was sick. Jessica Crews offered to come over after school and bring him soup. By eighth period, he was back in the nurse's office, a thermometer sticking out of his mouth.

"It's probably just stress," the nurse concluded when his temperature came up normal. "You kids are under a lot of pressure these days. Things were a lot simpler when I was your age."

Jax had to agree.

He found no relief at home. The visions were virtually back-to-back, and the PIP images were pretty much constant. At times they overlapped, two or three at once, filling his field of vision with so much input that he could barely see well enough to walk around his own apartment. How was he supposed to live like this? *You'll learn to cope,* Mako had assured him. But how would *he* know? The director himself had said that no one had ever been able to hypnotize remotely before. This was totally uncharted territory.

As terrible as Jax felt, he struggled to maintain the appearance that he was 100 percent okay. He couldn't let his parents see that he was suffering. He would never be so reckless as to tell them about the blowback, obviously. Still, the more they looked into what might be wrong with their son, the greater the chance that some word of it might get back to Dr. Mako. The director might misinterpret that as Jax betraying him. So he smiled a lot, which made his face contort into a hideous leer. He even hummed a little tune, which was risky. He'd never hummed much before. Would his parents notice the change in behavior?

"Someone's in a good mood," his mother observed.

"Aced my English exam," he lied, forcing a grin that would not have been out of place on someone who was being stretched on the rack.

Dad was at his laptop, searching flights to Florida for spring break. He was grumbling about airfares and schedules when, suddenly, Jax heard his own voice coming from the small office.

Frowning, he peered over his father's shoulder. His eyes, larger than life, stared back at him, morphing from violet to aquamarine.

". . . You will remember nothing of me or this message. Life will continue as usual. But the next time you operate the lever of a voting booth . . ."

Jax knew that his video message was making the rounds — the blowback alone proved that. But seeing the clip on the family computer as Ashton Opus browsed travel sites brought home the universal spread of the virus. And this was just day one! The election was more than a week away. How bad was this going to get?

"Dad —?" he ventured hesitantly.

His father didn't hear him. He was bent, his attention riveted on the huge eyes on the screen.

I just hypnotized my own father.

It was his dad's worst fear, rooted deep in his childhood with Opus parents. Jax searched his mind for the mesmeric impression that came from his father, but it was becoming impossible to pinpoint a single PIP amid the fog of blowback.

The message concluded and the pop-up disappeared from the computer, revealing flight schedules to Miami and Fort Lauderdale.

A shiver ran across his father's shoulders. "Oh, hi, Jax. I didn't see you standing there."

"Have you been looking for flights all this time?" Jax cleared his throat carefully. "Nothing else came up?"

"Just the fares," Dad replied sourly. "Remind me never to travel on a school break. Talk about extortion. There ought to be a law."

"Maybe there will be," Jax suggested. "We'll elect

a new president this fall. Who do you like in the primary?"

Ashton Opus did not even hesitate. "Oh, Douglas, definitely. And not only because we met him at Sentia. He just seems like the kind of man you pull that lever for."

25

The visions slackened around midnight, which gave Jax some hope that he'd be able to sleep. But it was not to be. He'd drift off for ten or fifteen minutes before some night owl — or someone in another time zone — would run into the video. The PIP would worm its way into a dream as if it belonged there. A garage door would open, a TV would switch on, a curtain would sweep aside, revealing two glowing, floating sprites — his own eyes. As with a real dream, he'd be able to go with it for a while, becoming increasingly aware that something was not quite right. And then he would awaken to a storm of blowback that would leave him shuddering.

As the week progressed, his time in school became a complete waste. He retained zero information from any classes; he barely heard his teachers. It was all he could do to keep his head upright as he sat there pretending to listen. Simultaneous visions blurred before him. It was impossible to keep count of how many. Having so much going on in his brain and in front of his eyes brought on waves of nausea, and he suffered pounding headaches. If it hadn't been for Tommy, he probably wouldn't have been able to navigate the halls.

On Friday, Jax caught a ride home with his father, and threw up all over the glove-leather interior of a quarter-million-dollar automobile. The Opuses had him at the pediatrician within an hour.

For all the misery that he was enduring, the loneliest part was that he didn't dare tell his parents what was happening to him. They'd insist on going to the police, which would expose them to grave danger from Dr. Mako. He couldn't look at them without thinking of the lethal post-hypnotic suggestion the director had implanted in them. It was as if Mom and Dad each carried a bomb with a hair trigger. Any wrong move by their son would certainly get them both killed.

So at the pediatrician's, he did what he had to do. He hypnotized Dr. DeSilva, and when that PIP superimposed itself over all the others, Jax spat out the tongue depressor and whispered, "I have a twenty-four-hour flu. It's nothing to worry about. And do you happen to know how to get the smell of barf out of a Bentley?"

He was gratified when the diagnosis came back. "Nothing to worry about. Just a twenty-four-hour bug. And for the car, I suggest a solution of white vinegar and water."

That fooled Mom and Dad for a while. But they knew how long twenty-four hours lasted, and days were going by with Jax getting worse instead of better. His skin was the color of parchment, and his eyes resembled Christmas tree ornaments, green irises surrounded by bloodshot red. The video had gone completely viral by that point, because there was rarely a moment where Jax wasn't weighed down by twenty, fifty, possibly even hundreds of PIP images. More proof: The opinion polls were showing Trey Douglas widening his lead over the hapless Governor Schaumberg. The election was the following Tuesday, and the experts were predicting a Douglas victory by a wide margin. Jax hadn't been to Sentia since the day he'd recorded the video clip, but he could almost hear Dr. Mako chortling with glee over the success of his scheme.

He should have been in bed, but he had to convince his parents he was getting better, so he forced himself to go out, volunteering for errands he never would have done if he'd truly felt fine. He couldn't get past the fruit market, where a dizzy spell sent him reeling into a pyramid of cantaloupes. In the end, Tommy had to take care of the post office and the library while Jax sat on a bench, holding a wad of damp paper towels to the back of his neck.

"Dude, is this ever going to end?"

Jax gazed at his friend through bleary eyes. "The election's over on Tuesday."

"Yeah, but the Internet goes on forever!" Tommy pointed out. "Maybe you should go to Sentia and ask Dr. Mako for help."

Jax regarded him sharply. "Why? Because he's devoted his life to New York City education and is an inspiration to every single one of us?"

"No, he's a rotten jerk, but he might know how you can live through this!"

"I wouldn't ask that guy for help if I was at death's door," Jax said stubbornly.

Tommy was worried. "How do you know you're not? What happens to people who can't sleep, and they don't eat because they can't keep anything down?"

"They puke in Bentleys," Jax replied sourly. "And let me tell you, my dad's boss had a few things to say about that."

"I'm serious, man!"

"You promised to get me to school the next two days," Jax reminded him. "I don't care if you have to carry me. My folks can't know that I'm not okay. Once the election's done, they'll pull the video. It might not happen right away, but surely the visions will taper off."

Monday was a nightmare. A hurricane of blowback raged all around him. He was aware of the school — the students and teachers — but it was as if he were a scuba diver, an alien visitor to a silent, murky world. If he hadn't had Tommy propping him up, he wasn't at all sure he could have managed to put one foot in front of the other.

Election Day dawned with a mixture of triumph and dread for Jax. He could see the light at the end of the tunnel — it would all be over soon. Yet he knew that the coming hours would bring the heaviest maelstrom of blowback yet. He made it through the morning in relatively good condition. He still couldn't keep food down, so he was weak with hunger. But he'd discovered through trial and error that drinking water kept him hydrated and a little more focused. At least he had the strength to make it up the big staircase to his sixth-period English class.

"Not bad, Opus —" Tommy began.

That was when the wave hit. Jax was far beyond individual PIPs at this point. What he felt was the ebb and flow of a current of disorientation. He knew an instant of vertigo and reached out for his friend to steady himself. Only Tommy had stepped to the other side of him on the landing. Jax was now draped over Rachel Herschiser, girlfriend of Butch Rockman, who was doing the eighth grade for the third time.

"Hey!"

The girl was ripped away from Jax, leaving him teetering on the brink with no one to hold on to.

Tommy leaped to interpose himself between his friend and the big boy. "Take it easy, Butch. He didn't mean anything by it —"

The shove had the power of a locomotive. Tommy staggered back, knocking Jax off the landing. Jax went down, striking every step along the way. It had to be a hallucination, but he saw — or thought he saw — the PIP images in his head being tossed around like the balls in a lotto machine. Then he hit bottom and saw nothing at all.

It was the most peace he'd had in a week.

26

Jax came back to himself in a place that definitely wasn't I.S. 222. A sharp antiseptic smell penetrated the never-ending gale of blowback. White walls, stainless steel . . . a hospital?

He sat up in bed, tugging on the IV in his arm. That explained why, in spite of everything, he felt pretty good. For days, nausea from the hypnotic onslaught had prevented him from keeping anything down. But he could be given fluids and nutrition directly through the tube.

Maybe Butch Rockman did me a favor. There's a first for everything.

Then he felt the back of his head and wished he hadn't. An egg-size lump under a soft gauze bandage, and pain to spare.

At least it's real, he reflected. Getting hurt was a reminder that, in spite of everything, the laws of science still applied to Jackson Opus. At this point, the bump on his head was practically the only thing anchoring him to the world.

He peered outside the blue curtain that surrounded his bed. Nurses and orderlies bustled around; gurneys rattled, and muted PA announcements could be heard. Jax was still in his school clothes, so he guessed this was Emergency. It was probably the best place for him on the day of the election, not that he could explain the nature of his emergency to any doctor.

He picked up the remote from the bedside table and switched on the TV that was mounted on the wall bracket. As he flipped channels, a headline in the CNN news crawl stopped his thumb.

EXIT POLLS POINT TO DOUGLAS LANDSLIDE IN NY DEM PRIMARY. . . . VICTORY WOULD CLINCH NOMINATION

Jax leaned back onto his head bump, which was agonizing even in contact with the soft pillow. No amount of blowback could distract his mind from the meaning of this news. Mako's plan was working. And, he, Jackson Opus, had been the key instrument that had made it so.

With one lousy video you've destroyed a system that's lasted more than two hundred years!

But what choice did he have, with his parents' lives hanging in the balance? Of course, history was filled with stories of heroes who had made devastating sacrifices for the good of the many.

I'm no hero.

He couldn't even comfort himself with the thought that, if he didn't cooperate, Mako would find somebody else. There *was* nobody else. He'd been in a unique position to stop this freight train in its tracks. Instead, he'd poured on more coal.

At the time, he'd followed the only path that made sense in order to protect his family. In the process, he'd subverted nothing less than the American system of democracy. And now that it was over, were Mom and Dad any safer? No! Mako hadn't removed the suggestion he'd implanted in them. They were in just as much danger as before. Maybe more, because now the director knew Jax could be blackmailed into anything in order to save the people he loved.

It almost tore Jax in two. He had more hypnotic ability than Mako. The director himself had said so. He should be able to overpower the man. But the one time he'd tried, he'd been slapped down like a pesky insect. His inexperience had held him back. And he'd never get any better, because the only person who could train him and develop his gift was Mako himself.

He was stuck. Nobody would ever take his side in this fight, because the whole world thought Elias Mako had devoted his life to New York City education and blah, blah, blah. There was not a single living soul who could see the director of Sentia for what he was.

When the answer came to Jax, it was like a sunrise bursting over the horizon, casting a glow even through the firestorm of hypnotic images that still battered him. There was one person who saw through Mako. Axel Braintree knew from the start that Mako was ruthless, dishonest, and dangerous. He'd tried to recruit Jax to be his spy at the institute. Jax had been stupid enough to rebuke him. Not anymore. Right now, the president of the Sandman's Guild was Jax's only hope.

"Oh, you're awake." A white-clad nurse burst in through his curtain. "You took a nasty fall. How are you feeling?"

"Pretty good," Jax lied. He swung a leg over the side of the bed. "In fact, I'm really anxious to get back to school —"

She pushed him back down with a hand that was gentle yet firm. "School will get along without you. Now" — she maneuvered the bed tray in front of him and dropped a thick sheaf of forms onto it — "I have some admissions paperwork for you to fill out."

"But I don't want to be admitted," Jax protested. "I want to be *released*."

"Well, you can't be discharged until you've been admitted," she reasoned, slapping a pen on top of the stack. "I'll check on you in a little while."

As soon as she was gone, Jax shoved the tray away, yanked the IV needle out of his arm, and kicked into his sneakers. The ER was busy; no one was going to notice a twelve-year-old with a bandaged head. His sole worry was his own nurse. Losing a patient with unfinished paperwork was probably a hanging offense at . . . he didn't even know which hospital this was.

He was almost home free, the door to the outside ten paces in front of him, when a half-demented voice shouted, "*Somebody grab that kid!*"

Two large orderlies started toward him, but Jax was already running. He blasted through the waiting room and out the automatic sliders. Blowback still battered and disoriented him, but he was pleased to note that the urgency of the moment was keeping him focused.

He found himself sprinting away from Beth Israel Medical Center, losing himself in the Union Square farmer's market. Over his shoulder, he saw the orderlies burst out of the building, look around, and turn back to the hospital. Apparently, he wasn't worth chasing, not even for the crime of un-filled-out forms.

This minor triumph energized him. Finally, something had gone right. Next order of business: Axel Braintree. The president of the Sandman's Guild had given him a card, but Jax had no idea what he'd done with it. His one connection to the man was the E-Z Wash Laundromat on Seventh Avenue, where the guild held its weekly gatherings.

It was about a fifteen-minute walk from Union Square. He entered the grimy storefront, brushing past the customers and their baskets, and barged into the back room where the meeting had been held.

Empty.

Okay, Jax told himself. *You knew this was a long shot. He still has to be somewhere.*

Jax had just resolved to return home and turn the apartment upside down looking for Braintree's business card, when he recognized the very tall woman at dryer number eight. She was a sandman . . . sandwoman? He'd seen her at the meeting — Evelyn Lolis, the one who used to make her living hypnotizing beauty-contest judges.

He rushed up to her. "I need to talk to Axel Braintree."

She fed quarters into the machine, never turning to face him. "Do I look like his mother?"

"I know you're in the Sandman's Guild. Please, it's an emergency."

She regarded him for the first time. "You're the Opus kid. What do you need Axel for?" She brightened. "You looking for a business partner?"

"It's about Elias Mako."

Ten seconds later, she had Braintree on her cell phone, and handed it to Jax.

Buffeted by blowback and embarrassed at how he'd dismissed the man before, Jax blurted out his message: "Mako rigged the election."

Braintree didn't ask "How?" or demand any supporting information. His response was immediate, and 100 percent to the point. "Where are you?"

"The Laundromat."

"Don't move," Braintree ordered. "I'll be there in ten minutes."

27

Jax would not have believed how glad he was to see the gray ponytail bouncing in through the Laundromat entrance.

Braintree himself was shocked at the sight of Jax — visibly thinner, very pale, with haunted bloodshot eyes. "What happened to you, kid? What did Mako do to you?"

Jax poured out the whole story, his voice cracking. Hearing the tale from day one was almost worse than living it. At least in reality, it all happened gradually. Recounting it was close to experiencing the entire nightmare in a few minutes.

"Remote hypnotism!" Braintree exclaimed in amazement. "Of course it's been *tried*, but no one's ever succeeded before! This changes everything we thought we knew about what it is to be a sandman!" He frowned. "But why do you look like you've just been released from a torture chamber?"

"I haven't been released," Jax quavered. "I'm still in it. You know how it kind of saps your strength when you've got a mesmeric link with somebody? Well, I've got a mesmeric link with everybody who sees that video clip! Hundreds of thousands of people, maybe more!"

"Of course!" Braintree was horrified. "The link would exist regardless of whether or not the hypnotism was performed in person! It must be overwhelming!"

Jax nodded miserably. "It feels like a regular link at first. But then you get so many at the same time that it's just a blur. Eventually it gets so bad that you can't eat, you can't sleep, you can barely walk. At this point, I can't tell if I feel so awful from the blowback, or the fact that I haven't had a decent meal or a good night's sleep in over a week — not to mention the knock on the head I got from falling down the stairs. It's not good!"

Braintree was alarmed. "You look terrible, but what really concerns me is that what you're going through is something no one has ever suffered before. We have no idea what the long-term damage might be. Maybe we should take you to a hospital."

Jax laughed mirthlessly. "I just escaped from one! What we have to do is find a way to stop Mako from hijacking the election, without bringing him down on my folks."

The old man glanced at the Laundromat clock, which was in the shape of a pair of sweat socks. "The polls close in a few hours. There's not much we can do to influence the voting now. We can work on thwarting him in the presidential election. But before we can do that, we have to make sure that your parents will be safe."

Neither of Jax's parents were answering their cell phones. Next, Jax tried calling them at work. The receptionist at the Bentley dealership said that Ashton Opus had to leave the office on a family emergency. "His son's in the hospital, you know."

Dr. Opus's chiropractic office had a recorded message explaining that the clinic was closed due to "unforeseen circumstances."

"They're at Beth Israel, trying to find me," Jax concluded. "I'm really not psyched to go back to that place. That nurse is probably still ticked off."

"Call your parents again," Braintree instructed. "Leave messages. Have them meet us at home. We have to act before Mako gets his hooks into them."

As the taxi bore them toward the Opuses' apartment, Jax had questions for the president of the Sandman's Guild. "How are we going to help them? Is it possible to undo what Dr. Mako did?"

"One step at a time," Braintree soothed. "We won't know that until we get inside their heads."

"My dad's going to flip," Jax groaned. "He's hated hypnotism his whole life. And my mom's in total denial. Wait till I show up with you to perform mental explorations and odd jobs."

"We'll be as quick as we can," the old man promised. "I suggest you put your mother under so she's not alarmed while I'm hypnotizing your father."

"Aw, I don't want to see inside my mother's brain. All those private thoughts and lady stuff. I get skeeved out just looking at her eyelash curler."

"Courage, Jax. Remember what we're doing it for."

The reception at home was overwhelming. Both parents were so relieved to see their son in one piece that any inconvenience and alarm was readily forgotten. Mrs. Opus enveloped Jax in a motherly hug, and Mr. Opus put his arm around his son's shoulder, whispering, "What's up with Farmer Ponytail?"

"Mom, Dad, I want you to meet Axel Braintree. He's . . . a friend of mine."

"Not from school, I guess," said his mother lamely.

"Delighted to meet you." Braintree handed each parent a business card.

Ashton Opus read, " 'Mental explorations'? Wait — you're not one of . . ." He would have said more, but the old man fixed him with a penetrating stare, and he was instantly in a trance.

It was the first time Monica Opus had ever witnessed hypnotism firsthand, and it scared her witless. She snatched up a crystal vase and wielded it like a weapon. "Get away from my husband, you —"

Jax leaped in front of her and fixed his dark eyes on hers.

"Jackson Howard Opus, don't you dare —"

That was as far as she got. Her PIP reflected back at him clearer than the chaotic jumble of pictures he continued to receive.

"Hurry up," he tossed over his shoulder. "When she comes out of it, she's going to kill me."

There was no response from the old man, who was deep in a mesmeric link with Mr. Opus. Jax may have had the stronger natural gift, but he had never seen a hypnotist so completely focused as Braintree. His attention shone like an interrogator's lamp on Dad, who seemed to be answering quietly. The head sandman had devoted his life and his guild to resisting the temptation to bend people. It was plain, though, that when he did it, he could be extremely good at it.

But is he good enough to undo the deadly suggestion Mako planted inside Dad? Is something like that even possible?

If this was unsuccessful, the consequences would be dire. And not just for Mom and Dad. For the first time, his thoughts turned to the terrible state of his own health — drawn and pale, gaunt and anxious. And who knew what was causing it all?

He pulled himself up short. Wait a minute! He knew *exactly* what was causing his current predicament!

These weren't *his* thoughts; they were *Mom's*! He was starting to pick up her emotions through the mesmeric link! The last thing a guy needed was to know his mother's innermost feelings.

He tried to close his mind a little, but felt the link wavering, so he abandoned that idea. Fine. If he couldn't keep out his mother's thoughts, at least he could distract himself so he wouldn't have to receive them.

O say, can you see, by the dawn's early light, what so proudly we hailed —

This patriotic anthem was interrupted by Braintree tapping him on the shoulder. Dad was waiting patiently, eyes half-closed, in hypnotic neutral.

"Well?" Jax hissed.

"I know what we're up against." The old man took a deep breath. "It's nasty, even for Mako."

Jax was deflated. "I was kind of hoping he was just bluffing."

"I won't mention the trigger word yet. It's too dangerous. When they hear it, both your parents will proceed to the nearest subway station and throw themselves in front of an uptown train."

Jax was overcome with rage and terror in the same instant. "What kind of monster comes up with something like that?"

"I told you, Dr. Mako is not what he seems. Except to me. To me he's always been unacceptable."

Unacceptable was not the term Jax would have chosen. "But you fixed it, right? Now we just have to do the same thing to Mom."

The president of the Sandman's Guild shook his head grimly. "I don't like Elias Mako, but his understanding of the inner machinery of the human mind is unparalleled. This cannot be fixed in the way you mean it."

Jax was appalled. "Why not? Can't we just put in a suggestion of our own? You know — when you hear the trigger word, *don't* jump in front of a subway train?"

"This is no simple hypnotic trick," Braintree explained. "Mako has managed to ingrain the suggestion into the basic foundation of your father's sense of himself. Even more dangerous, he seems to have built in a safeguard against any countersuggestion we might make. I'm not sure exactly how it works, but if we try to override Mako's handiwork, it might have the reverse effect of setting it all off."

Jax was in a panic. "You mean there's *nothing* we can do? That means I'm Mako's slave forever or else my parents die!"

"I wouldn't go that far," the old man assured him. "If all the conditions of Mako's hypnotic command can be met, then the suggestion will disappear. You can only die once, after all."

Jax was distraught. "But they'll be dead!"

"The art of suggestion is very literal," Braintree lectured. "That's why sandmen make lousy Little League coaches. You tell a kid to steal a base, and he sticks it under his shirt and runs for the parking lot."

The link with Mrs. Opus was flickering in and out. If Jax didn't concentrate, she'd be awake in a moment, and none too pleased with her son.

"But how could anybody misinterpret *throw yourself in front of a train*?" Jax challenged.

"You're going to have to trust me."

"The last person I trusted was Mako."

"I'm not Mako."

"No," Jax agreed. "You're a convicted art thief who holds self-help meetings in a Laundromat."

"But do you trust me?" Braintree persisted.

And Jax was amazed to discover that he did.

28

The first part of Braintree's plan was to start the Opuses on the path to killing themselves. In other words, they had to deliberately trigger Dr. Mako's post-hypnotic suggestion.

Even though Jax accepted that this was the only way to defuse the time bomb inside his parents, it was an agonizing decision. After all, at this moment, Mr. and Mrs. Opus were just fine. The notion of setting them on a course designed to murder them — on purpose — was unimaginably terrifying.

"You do it," Jax told Braintree. "I might not have the guts."

The two sandmen brought Jax's parents out of their hypnotic state. Jax was still so disoriented by blowback that he neglected to instruct his mother to forget recent events, and she came back to herself still angry. "How dare you bring this witch doctor into our home and set him on your father? Just because you happen to have a talent for hypnotism, it doesn't give you the right to . . ."

He was so cowed by her onslaught that he overcame his fear and nodded to Braintree to give the trigger word. It might be the only way to stop her diatribe.

"Lusitania," the old man announced, enunciating carefully.

Jax had expected at least a thunderclap and frantic action from Mom and Dad. But it was all very civilized. Mrs. Opus straightened her hair and picked up her pocketbook. Her husband adjusted his tie. Wordlessly, the Opuses shrugged into their jackets and headed out of the building to die.

Jax and Braintree followed a few steps behind them.

"I can't believe they're so *calm* about it," Jax whispered. "Like they're going out to pick up a loaf of bread."

Braintree nodded. "The response to a post-hypnotic suggestion is always very businesslike."

"Yeah, but they're going to kill themselves!"

"They're responding to a series of specific instructions," Braintree amended. "And that's how we'll save their lives."

A neighbor greeted Jax's parents as they crossed the street at the corner. The Opuses looked right through her and kept on walking. There was a tense moment at the next intersection when a changing light separated the couple, and Braintree and Jax hesitated, unsure of who would stick with whom. In the confusion, Mr. Opus ended up a block ahead, with both sandmen tailing his wife. Frantic, Jax sprinted ahead, reacquiring the faint bald spot that was his father. A stalled delivery truck snarled pedestrian traffic, allowing Mrs. Opus and Braintree to catch up.

Jax could see it at the end of the block — the entrance

to the Canal Street subway station. He swallowed hard, willing himself to concentrate through his continuing whirlwind of mesmeric images. Whatever was going to happen, it would happen there.

"Stick with your father, no matter what," the old man commanded. "I'll look after your mom."

Jax could feel a lump of ice in his stomach as he watched his parents descending the concrete steps into the station. It looked so ordinary and everyday that it was hard to accept what was coming. Jax was used to hypnotism now, even good at it. But nothing could have prepared him for this life-and-death moment.

The Opuses swiped their cards and entered the station, Braintree following close behind them. Jax made for the turnstile . . .

And froze.

At this critical instant, every move planned down to split seconds, a dumb mistake was tipping the scale toward tragedy. His MetroCard was on his dresser at home! His eyes darted to the fare booth; there was a long line. By the time he got through, at least one of his parents would be gone.

Without hesitation, Jax vaulted over the barrier and ran for the flight of stairs down to the platform. A hand grabbed him by the shoulder and pulled him back. He spun around to face a burly transit cop.

"What's the matter, kid? You're too special to pay your fare like everybody else?"

"I — I — I —" A plea was forming in his throat, but at that moment, he felt the earthquake-like rumble of a train approaching the station. Even if he could come up with the right words, there'd be no time to save Mom and Dad!

He stared at the man with laser-straight intensity, trying to conjure centuries of Opus and Sparks history into one mesmeric blast. The cop recoiled slightly, and then sagged, motionless. Jax shrugged out of his grasp and sprinted for the stairs. As he flung himself off the bottom step, he could feel the blast of air coming from the tunnel just ahead of the train. The sight he beheld nearly stopped his heart.

Mom stood on the yellow safety stripe, poised for flight. Braintree was right behind her, looking around wildly for Jax. His desperation needed no explanation. He could save one, but not both.

Heart hammering, Jax scoured the platform. At that instant, he was aware of no blowback. The entire universe had been distilled to a single, vitally important question: *Where's Dad?*

The squeal of brakes from the oncoming train was deafening now. The headlights raked across the station.

At the very last instant, Jax spied the familiar bald spot, standing at the edge about twenty feet beyond Mom.

Jax took a mad dash in the direction of his doomed father. The front of the train burst out of the tunnel. Dad crouched slightly, preparing his jump.

"No-o-o-o!"

Jax left his feet in a flying tackle. As he clamped both arms around his father's midsection, he felt Dad's momentum pulling both of them over the edge. Still in midair, he heaved away from the onrushing train. The two of them hit the concrete, rolling back from the gap as hundreds of tons of metal screamed into the station. Out of the corner of his eye, as his cheek struck the platform, he caught sight of Braintree, a screaming Monica Opus locked up against a trash bin.

Dad was weeping and moaning piteously, pounding his fists against his son's chest and shoulders. To Jax, this was almost as upsetting as the near-miss with the train. He had never seen his father so much as sniffle with emotion, much less fall completely to pieces.

A crowd of onlookers was beginning to gather around them, but Jax barely noticed.

Braintree hustled Mrs. Opus over to her husband and son. Mom was weeping, and Dad's face was a mask of horror.

"What's wrong with them?" Jax asked.

"They're experiencing what it is to give up your life," Braintree whispered.

"But they're *fine* . . ." Jax protested. He noticed a bloody scrape on his father's chin. It was probably painful.

But imagine the damage if I hadn't done it!

The train shuddered to a stop and its doors opened. Passengers got on and off, and the curious around them dispersed. One man offered to dial 9-1-1. He seemed relieved, though, when Braintree assured him there was no need.

The Opuses were still shaken, but allowed themselves to be seated side by side on a bench.

"Shouldn't we get them out of here?" Jax intoned anxiously. "How do we know they won't just try to jump in front of the *next* train?"

"They're not in danger anymore," the head sandman said. "They've complied with the suggestion."

"Are you sure?" Jax probed. "We stopped them at the last minute."

"That's exactly why it had to be at the last minute. A suggestion is like a hypnotic contract. To fulfill the contract, they were required to throw themselves off the platform in front of a train. They did that. The fact that we pulled them back is irrelevant. They're free."

With the imminent crisis past, Jax experienced a surge of relief accompanied by a wallop of blowback that nearly knocked him over.

I guess that's the antidote, he thought with a pained half smile. *When you're scared out of your wits, you don't notice how miserable you are.*

The other platform began to rumble and the screeching roar signaled the arrival of the uptown express. The noise seemed to startle the Opuses back to themselves. Despite Braintree's assurances, Jax was mightily thrilled that his parents didn't try to rush over to the opposite track for another shot at Mako's command.

Mr. Opus shook himself like a wet dog. "What are we doing in the subway? We have a Bentley!"

"They're cleaning it, Dad," Jax reminded him. "The barf, remember?"

"We couldn't find you at the hospital," Mrs. Opus recalled. "And you met us at home with that awful man who attacked your father —"

"Farmer Ponytail!" her husband added.

Braintree stepped forward. "I'm still here."

"His name is Axel Braintree, and he just saved your lives — both of you," Jax informed them.

"There are a lot of things you have to know," said the old man. "Let's find a place we can talk."

At a bagel shop near the subway station, the Opuses listened to the story, their expressions growing more flabbergasted and awestruck with each new detail. Jax's power of remote hypnotism; the deadly suggestion to ensure his cooperation; the video virus; the storm of blowback that still assaulted their son; and, most appalling of all, Mako's scheme to plant his puppet in the Oval Office.

"I — I can't believe it," Mr. Opus managed faintly. "Dr. Elias Mako has devoted his life to New York City education and is an inspiration to every single one of us!"

"No, he's not," Jax said gently. "He *bent* you to think that — probably while he was implanting the suggestion to make you jump in front of a train. He's a bad guy, Dad. I mean, like, Voldemort bad."

His mother was nearly as pale as her son, teeth chattering against her heavy coffee mug. "We have to go to the police," she insisted. "If what you say is true, someone just tried to *murder* us!"

"No police!" her husband said sharply. "Maybe I've tried to forget my whole childhood, but if there's one thing

I remember from my parents, it's this: *Never* mention hypnotism to the authorities. Too many Opuses already have spent their lives in straitjackets and rubber rooms."

"Besides," Jax added, "the mayor and the police commissioner are both on Mako's wall of shame. They're probably as much under his thumb as Senator Douglas."

"So we just do *nothing*?" she demanded in outrage. "We nearly *died*! Our son is stumbling around like he's got the plague! Someone is trying to hijack our entire political system!"

The fourth person at the table, the president of the Sandman's Guild, chewed thoughtfully on a whole-wheat raisin bagel. "There is one thing we might be able to do." The others regarded him expectantly. "Mako controls Trey Douglas through mesmerism. But the senator would be just as vulnerable to any sandman, especially one as powerful as Jax."

Jax blinked. "You think I can out-hypnotize Mako and take Douglas away from him?"

"Well," Braintree replied, "it's not as simple as that —"

"You bet it's not!" Jax exclaimed. "I tried to bend Mako once, and he wrecked me!"

"That's to be expected," the old man assured him. "You only learned what you can do a matter of months ago; he's been developing and honing his skills for decades. Look no further than your ability to hypnotize remotely to understand the extent of your power. You are very large potatoes."

Jax was bitter. "Every week, you get up in your

Laundromat and preach about resisting the temptation to hypnotize, but I have to go out and bend a US senator?"

"That's because you are unique among our kind, Jackson Opus," Braintree replied readily. "Most sandmen your age would be mesmerizing teachers and prom dates or getting into movies without paying. But you honestly have no interest in personal gain. Your talent is unequaled, and so are you."

"And what a rich reward I'm getting for it," Jax added sarcastically. "Enough blowback to put me in the hospital, and an evil genius gunning for my parents."

"Greatness is a burden," the old man acknowledged. "I wish I could do this for you but, unlike you, I can't be trusted with vast power. My experience with the Department of Corrections is proof of that. I can only use my skill for a limited time before the world begins to resemble a fabulous mall where all the price tags read *free*. If I hypnotize Trey Douglas, how do I know I could resist the temptation to be just as bad as Mako? You alone can be relied upon to do the right thing — to bend the senator and compel him to drop out of the race."

Monica Opus had heard enough. "If Elias Mako is going to be there, I don't want Jax anywhere near the place. That man has seen the last of our family. I don't care if he gets a pink poodle elected president! He's never going to have the chance to hurt us again!"

"That garbage barge is already loading in Yonkers," the head sandman said gravely. "Mako will need Jax again for the general election in the fall, and threatening you two will still be the best way to make him cooperate. Our only hope is to put a stop to it tonight."

"Now just one minute," Mr. Opus spoke up. "I know a lot of these hotshot political types from the dealership. They don't even go to the bathroom without an entourage. Now that Douglas has clinched the nomination, he'll have Secret Service, too. No one's going to be able to get near him."

Braintree nodded reluctantly. "I hate to break my own rules. But this is going to take hypnotism."

"You're talking about a twelve-year-old kid!" Jax's father persisted. "Even if he's got you helping him, there's no way he could get around all that security."

The old man produced his cell phone and scrolled through a very full contact list. "Luckily, I happen to know a lot of very frustrated sandmen who would jump at the chance to use their talents for a worthy cause. And if a couple of wallets go missing, or the occasional Rolex, it's a small price to pay for saving our democracy."

29

Senator Douglas's press conference was scheduled for nine o'clock that night. It was very big news, since his enormous win in New York State gave him more than enough delegates to clinch the Democratic presidential nomination. All TV stations were covering his speech live. The street in front of the Hotel Galaxy was a parking lot of network news trucks. Reporters spoke into microphones, setting up the mammoth event. At every entrance, dark-suited watchful men spoke into headsets, panning the crowd of thousands surrounding the building.

A half hour before, the nominee himself had arrived at the hotel in a stretch limo with bulletproof glass. Senator Douglas was accompanied by his family, his closest campaign advisors, and a tall hawk-nosed man who was recognized by few in the crowd. The TV stations identified him as the director of a New York–based institute known as Sentia. Name: Elias Mako.

"Look at him," muttered Axel Braintree at the back of the crowd. He turned to Ivan Marcinko, the disgraced electronics salesman. "Do you see what happens when hypnotism and blind ambition are allowed to mix?"

"Doesn't seem so bad to me," Marcinko commented. "He's a big shot being chauffeured around in a fancy car."

"Not bad for a Cadillac, I guess," Mr. Opus began. "We do an elegant stretch with —" He stopped himself abruptly. He wasn't a Bentley representative tonight. The next few hours could very well determine the Opuses' future, including whether they lived or died. Nothing could be more serious than that.

The high stakes were certainly getting to Monica Opus. She was a strong woman and a no-nonsense person. As a chiropractor, she was used to being able to look at an X-ray and know exactly what needed to be done — a spinal adjustment, for example. Before this roller-coaster ride, she'd never even heard of the great hypnotist bloodlines, much less realized that she was descended from one and had married into another. That her family was in danger was difficult enough; the notion that their fate was bound up in a paranormal mental power she couldn't begin to imagine was almost impossible for her to accept.

She turned to Jax. "Where are all the sandmen? You said there was a whole guild."

Only Marcinko and tall Evelyn Lolis, the dethroned beauty queen, had arrived so far.

"They'll be here, Mom." Jax wished he could be as confident as Braintree, who seemed totally unfazed by the fact that his hypnotist army hadn't shown up yet.

One positive note: Jax was almost himself again. As soon as voting ended for the New York primary, Dr. Mako must have pulled the plug on the video virus. The flood of blowback was already down to a trickle. And while Jax still grappled with a few random images, it was a breeze compared with what he'd endured over the past week. In a couple of days, the self-erasing virus would likely disappear from the Internet, and he would be back to normal.

If there's such a thing as normal for me after tonight.

But all things considered, he felt pretty good. Actually, what he really felt was *hungry*. With the headaches and nausea gone, his appetite was coming back with a vengeance.

Too bad they're not holding this press conference in a steak house!

Jax checked his phone. There was a text from Tommy: *Where are you, man? The hospital says you ran out on the bill! What gives?*

It was eight forty. Security was already letting Douglas's campaign workers into the ballroom. Where were the sandmen?

And then they began to arrive, from subway entrances, off buses, out of taxicabs. They parked their cars, chained up their bikes, and hefted skateboards under their arms. They were all ages, shapes, and sizes. Some wore business suits, others ripped jeans and faded T-shirts. One was clad in the robes and sandals of a Franciscan friar, complete with a tonsured head. As a group, there was nothing to differentiate the newcomers from anyone else in the crowd. Yet Jax would have been able to pick them out in a ninety-thousand-seat stadium. They had what could only be described as *that look*. It was a mixture of confidence and secrecy, with just a dash of devil-may-care. Or maybe it was the fact that they studiously avoided looking anyone straight in the eye.

The throng undulated around them as they converged on Axel Braintree. How many were there? At first, Jax counted a dozen. But, no, they kept coming. Mr. and Mrs. Opus watched as the odd assortment of characters reported in. There must have been at least thirty of them. Soon Braintree stood at the center of a motley collection of individuals waiting for his instructions.

"These are the hypnotists we're depending on to save us?" Mrs. Opus hissed. "They're straight out of the cantina scene in *Star Wars*!"

"You should have seen my parents' wedding album," her husband told her.

"You never showed it to me."

He was triumphant. "Exactly."

With a pleased expression, Braintree briefed his troops on the operation to rescue American democracy. "How about this turnout?" he boasted. "If you'd show this kind of effort coming to meetings, we'd have a lot more satisfied parole officers in this city."

There was a half annoyed, half ashamed murmur from the sandmen, and a few of them looked at their watches. So Braintree soldiered on. "Security will be very tight. Don't be overconfident. This is the Secret Service. If you've never hypnotized through sunglasses before, it can be tricky, since you can't be sure the subject is looking at you.

And remember, just because you've bent one agent doesn't mean his partner won't come after you.

"The goal is to get Jax close enough to hypnotize Trey Douglas before he makes his acceptance speech," the old man continued. "But, obviously, any of you who gets a crack at the senator should take it. Keep the suggestion simple: *I'm happy to get the nomination. Thanks but no thanks. I'm dropping out of the race.* Don't get fancy. Mako's had his hooks in this guy for years, so who knows what mesmeric safeguards could be built in. I also want two sandmen on Ashton and Monica —"

"Sand*persons*," Lolis interrupted the guild president.

"Thanks, Evelyn. That'll be your job, yours and — yes — Ivan's. Mako can't know they're here. He's already tried to hurt them once."

The doors opened and security began to usher the spectators inside, passing each one through a metal detector.

"There's not going to be room for all these people," Jax observed nervously. "What if we don't get in?"

Braintree smiled patiently. "Obviously, that's not going to be a problem for *us*."

It was impressive to watch the sandmen operate. As they swarmed toward the doors, regular people backed off to let them pass. When the Franciscan friar was pulled aside by one security man, a quick face-to-face changed the agent's mind. There was no question that Braintree's troops were hypnotizing their way inside with an almost military precision.

As Jax stepped through the metal detector, he became aware that four sandmen were surrounding him, clearing his path to the ballroom. The lobby was an atrium, soaring fourteen stories high, framed by stripes of mezzanines on three sides and, over the magnificent entrance, acres of diaphanous gold drapery covering, but not obscuring, a wall of windows. He looked around, trying to catch a glimpse of his parents. He couldn't see them, and hoped this was because Lolis and Marcinko were keeping them safely back and out of sight.

His momentum carried him through the magnificent French doors and into the ballroom, where a jubilant crowd was celebrating the New York primary victory that had clinched the nomination for their man. Trey Douglas signs were everywhere, splashed across the walls, and waved and carried by supporters. Jax craned his neck, peering over heads, placards, flashing cameras, and microphones. The stage was wrapped with red, white, and blue bunting. It was empty at the moment, but chairs had been set up flanking a podium, complete with a teleprompter.

As they approached the front, the crowd grew louder and more raucous, tightening in density as everyone pushed forward. Progress became more difficult, and Jax's escorts began hypnotizing audience members to step aside. Jax couldn't help noticing sandman William Durbin removing a fat wallet from an onlooker's breast pocket as he advanced Jax another space. He was about to say something when he realized that the crisis of the moment far outweighed a single case of minor thievery. A few feet ahead, a woman's gold bracelet disappeared under the friar's rough brown robes. Okay, *several* cases of thievery, some of them not so minor. Braintree was watching from near the back, frowning his disapproval. The old man had been right, Jax reflected. The sandmen needed all the meetings they could get to.

There was a roar of excitement as the platform party filed onto the stage and took their seats. Jax ducked his head behind Durbin's broad shoulders. There was Mako, right in the middle of everything. But . . . where was Trey Douglas? Surely the nominee-to-be wasn't planning to sit out his own victory celebration.

Durbin read his mind. "The big cheese never comes out till the last minute. Haven't you ever heard of a grand entrance?" He took advantage of the crowd's distraction to help himself to another wallet.

"Cut it out!" Jax breathed.

Shamefaced, the sandman slipped the billfold back into the satchel it had come from.

Durbin was right about the program. The order of business seemed to be to rev the spectators up to fever pitch before the man of the hour showed his face. Douglas's campaign manager got the ball rolling, before handing over the podium to a couple of government bigwigs, who passed the baton to the candidate's wife and his two stalwart sons. By this time, the energy level in the ballroom threatened to blow the roof clean off the building. People were bouncing up and down, cheering, dancing, and waving their arms. What they *weren't* doing was looking into the eyes of the sandmen who were hypnotizing their way to the front, bearing Jax with them.

Jax began to panic. Mrs. Douglas was about to introduce her husband. Jax had to be close enough to lock eyes with the nominee before the guy turned his attention to the prompter and began his speech.

The sandmen had shifted their strategy from hypnotizing to good old-fashioned pushing. Jax joined the crush, trying to ram his shoulder between two onlookers to open up a pathway. He bounced right off them.

Mrs. Douglas's high-pitched voice penetrated the farthest corners of the space. "I'm proud to introduce the man I love, the man all of America will soon love. My husband and our next president, *Trey Douglas*!"

And there he was, Elias Mako's puppet, Senator Trey Douglas, greeting his supporters with his double-white smile and thirty-two teeth prominently displayed. The crowd erupted into insanity. Confetti fluttered and balloons dropped from the ceiling. A brass band blared out some obscure college-football fight song, but nobody could hear it anyway. The din was nothing short of earsplitting.

Unable to move a single inch forward, Jax leaped as high as he could in a futile attempt to capture Douglas's attention. At last, he hoisted himself up on the shoulders of two of the sandmen.

"Senator — over here!"

It was no use. Douglas was hugging his wife and sons, shaking hands, always looking in the wrong direction.

"Senator!"

And suddenly, the nominee's eyes drifted over to the boy who was above the crowd.

Jax's heart surged. *This is it!* But before he could lock on, a tall, lean body stepped in front of the candidate and glared out over the sea of faces.

Mako!

Jax dropped back to the floor, rebuffed. The enemy knew he was here, and would guard Douglas with his full arsenal of hypnotic tricks. There was no way for Jax to fight back. The Sentia director was too experienced and too strong.

How am I going to bend Douglas now?

The taste of defeat was bitter in his mouth. It was over. The candidate was already stepping up to the podium. In another minute, the combined power of every Opus and Sparks who'd ever lived wouldn't be enough to reach the guy. His focus would be strictly on the teleprompter.

You can't very well hypnotize someone who isn't looking at you.

Unless . . .

Suddenly, Jax was on the go again — not forward, but sideways through the crowd.

"Come back, man!" Durbin shouted over the noise. "There's still a chance!"

Jax was already committed to this new course of action. There was no way he could get close enough to the stage in time. Yet maybe, just maybe, he could make it to the tech station at the side of the ballroom. It housed the main switchboard that controlled lights and sound. Jax wasn't interested in those features. His destination was the computer that fed the teleprompter on the podium.

Lateral movement — away from the stage — was a lot easier than trying to bull forward. He caught a bewildered look from Braintree, but pushed on. There was no time for explanations. Ducking low to avoid waving arms and signs, he burrowed through the revelers and slipped under the cordon that surrounded the control center.

"Hey, you're not allowed —"

Jax turned his eyes on the man, silencing his protest. One by one, he mesmerized the technical crew. For most, it took no more than a piercing glance. For others, a simple command was required: "Stand back and do nothing." To the woman at the computer, he said, "You have to go to the bathroom. It's urgent."

When she got up and ran, he took her chair.

"Thank you! Thank you very much!" Douglas was at the microphone. The ovation was dying down as the audience readied itself for the candidate's words.

If Jax didn't act now, it would be too late — for himself, his parents, maybe even the entire country.

He looked at the screen of the laptop and saw the words: *MY FRIENDS, WE GATHER TONIGHT IN OUR NATION'S LARGEST CITY TO CELEBRATE THE BEGINNING OF A MOVEMENT THAT WILL BE FELT IN EVERY TOWN AND VILLAGE FROM SEA TO SHINING . . .*

In a flash, Jax realized how the system functioned.

Whatever was on the computer would be projected onto the teleprompter in front of the candidate. Right now, it was the nominee's acceptance speech.

But not for long . . .

His finger trembling as it moved on the touchpad, Jax activated the laptop's webcam and stared straight into the lens. He had no idea if this would work. Every mind-bender he'd ever known or studied had used speech to deliver mesmeric commands. He had no way to speak to his subject here. All he had was a keyboard.

Here goes nothing, he thought.

Standing at the podium, basking in the adoration of the crowd at the greatest moment in his political career, Senator Trey Douglas watched his speech disappear from the teleprompter. The words he had rehearsed so diligently were replaced by a huge pair of remarkable eyes, changing in color from green to blue to purple and back again. It confused him at first that at this vitally important point in his life, nothing should seem as urgent as looking into those eyes.

A long, narrow pop-up appeared below the face. A message crawled across the prompter:

YOU ARE VERY RELAXED.

And he *was*! *Completely* relaxed. He'd never been so completely at peace in his life, and it was all thanks to those wonderful eyes!

Another message appeared:

READY FOR YOUR SPEECH?

Onstage, Douglas squared his shoulders and nodded vigorously. It looked a little peculiar, but his ecstatic supporters assumed it was just the candidate being caught up in the excitement of the moment.

Seated at the computer in the tech booth, Jax was in complete control. After enduring a blur of hundreds of thousands of cascading images, now there was only one. He focused all his concentration on it, knowing that Douglas was completely in his hands. As he typed, he heard his words coming from the candidate himself over the public address system.

"My friends, thank you for this honor of being your candidate for president of the United States. Unfortunately, I've decided to drop out of the race. . . ."

A titanic gasp sucked every molecule of air out of the ballroom. The silence that followed was so total that it would have been possible to hear the six footsteps of an ant walking across the floor.

Onstage behind the senator, Elias Mako leaped to his feet, his face a mask of shock and horror. Past Douglas's left ear, he spotted Jackson Opus's unique eyes staring out of the teleprompter. His fevered brain toyed briefly with the idea of hypnotizing Douglas back to himself and trying to pass the episode off as a joke. But he knew in his heart it wouldn't wash. This "speech" was being beamed around the world over dozens of TV and radio networks, the Internet, and every form of social media. This disaster was only a handful of seconds old, yet it was already too late.

His vision clouded by rage, he fixed his gaze on the tech station and saw exactly the person he expected to see. The sole person capable of accomplishing this act of remote hypnotism. *The one Mako himself had shown how it could be done!*

"I hope you're not too bummed about this," the former candidate went on in an apologetic tone, "but I guess you're going to have to nominate somebody else. Bye."

Typing furiously, Jax gave his final instruction:

WHEN MY EYES DISAPPEAR, YOU WILL REMEMBER NOTHING OF THE PAST TWO MINUTES.

And he yanked the power cord out of the floor outlet.

Douglas stepped back from the podium and turned to his good friend and supporter, Dr. Mako. "Well, how did I do?"

In the dead silence, his words could be heard in every corner of the ballroom. They didn't seem to make sense.

The quiet lasted a grand total of eight seconds. Then, mayhem. The camera flashes were blinding, the babble of shouted questions just an unintelligible din. Every reporter in the hotel made a bull run for the ex-candidate, determined to score the scoop of the century. The traffic jam was unimaginable — media swarming and devastated campaign workers screaming *"Why? Why? Why?"* Shoving matches broke out; punches were thrown; the sandmen circulated through the chaos helping themselves to wallets and handbags faster than Axel Braintree could stop them.

The old man was outnumbered, and his flock was in a feeding frenzy.

In all the disorder, Jax came face-to-face with Elias Mako.

The director was in a towering rage. His crimson face radiated heat. "There will be payback!" he spat, tight-lipped.

"Jax!" came a voice behind them.

Jax wheeled. Talk about bad timing. His parents were pushing their way toward him, Lolis and Marcinko struggling to keep up. He should have known this would happen. There was no way Mom and Dad would cool their heels outside with a riot going on and Jax in the middle of it.

"Get out of here!" Jax ordered, waving them away.

It was too late. Mako had spotted them. "Now you'll see that actions have consequences!" He spun in their direction and hurled a single word. "Lusitania!"

There was no reaction from the Opuses.

Mako must have believed that they simply hadn't heard him amid the ruckus. He jumped back onstage, rushed to the microphone, and shouted, *"Lusitania!"* The ballroom echoed with his command.

Mrs. Opus frowned. "What's he yelling about?"

Jax saw red. Yes, the post-hypnotic suggestion had been defused. But Mako didn't know that!

He's trying to murder them for revenge!

In a rage, he turned his powerful eyes on Mako. He had no idea what he intended to do — hypnotize him? Punch him? Curse him out? All of the above? He wasn't sure. He couldn't see beyond the fact that his hatred of this evil man had to take some form.

Too late he realized that he had let his mind wander, and by the time he returned to focus, he was under attack. It was no mere stirring in the brain, but powerful robot arms tearing into his innermost thoughts.

Desperately, Jax tried to muster his defenses against the assault, only to understand that he was completely outgunned. Days of debilitating blowback had weakened him, and the teleprompter-bending of Trey Douglas had sapped what little hypnotic power he had left. There was no defending against an adversary with the skill and experience of Sentia's director.

Mako stepped down from the rostrum and approached slowly, his expression intense, yet calm.

Fight back, Jax exhorted himself. *You're stronger than he is! You can keep him out!*

A calm voice very close by said, "Why would you resist? It's so much more pleasant to let yourself go."

Never!

"You are very relaxed . . . very comfortable. . . ."

No!

A moment later, Jax couldn't understand what he was so upset about. He was *fine.* Come to think of it, he'd never felt better in his life. Energized, well rested — happy, even. The remnants of his deluge of hypnotic blowback were gone. In fact, he could barely remember the weeklong onslaught . . . a vague recollection of something disagreeable in the very distant past . . . What was it again . . . ?

"Isn't this nice?" asked Mako.

"Mmm," Jax murmured, "great." Why would anyone resist something so wonderful? What had he been thinking? Jax couldn't imagine fighting against this bliss. All that mattered was to keep it going. . . .

"This glorious feeling can be with you always," Mako promised, and Jax knew in his heart that it was 100 percent true. "But there's something important you have to do first."

"Of course," Jax promised aloud. "Anything."

"Now listen carefully. . . ."

31

In the middle of the roiling crowd, Axel Braintree snatched the phone from the friar's hand and dropped it into its real owner's pocket.

"Have a heart, Axel! The pickings haven't been this good since the Yankees' last ticker-tape parade!"

"Control yourself, Tuck," Braintree hissed. "Do you want to go back on house arrest?"

"Kiyoko's got more stuff than me. How come you're not giving her a hard time?"

Sure enough, there was another sandman a few yards away, digging inside someone's backpack.

Braintree rushed off, sternly tossing over his shoulder, "I'm not finished with you yet!" What a night! Obviously, he was thrilled that they'd managed to thwart Mako's plan to place a puppet president in the Oval Office. But who could have predicted that his sandmen would go wild in a crowd so big? This represented months of progress down the drain! It was going to be hard to get them back to the Laundromat for more meetings. He might have to bring back Donut Night after all. . . .

He had almost reached Kiyoko when Evelyn Lolis

grabbed him by the arm. "I'm worried about the boy," she called over the noise of the crowd.

He followed her pointing finger. There was Jax, making his way to the door, striding purposefully.

"He's probably taking a bathroom break," Braintree told her. "He's earned it. He just saved the world, you know."

Lolis shook her head. "He's coming off a face-to-face with Mako. I think he's bent."

The old man was instantly alert. Jax had thrown a monkey wrench into the Sentia director's greatest ambitions. His revenge would be terrible.

Showing remarkable agility for a man his age, Braintree darted through the milling throng and followed Jax out to the hotel atrium.

"Wait up, kid!" he called. Louder: "Jax, you did it!"

Jax gave no sign that he'd heard, although the words echoed around the fourteen-story lobby. He continued to cross the atrium with long, determined strides.

The old man broke into a run. The crowd was thinner here. All the action was inside the ballroom.

The Opuses appeared in the entranceway. "Jax?" his mother called. "Where are you going?"

There was no response. Jax stepped inside the chrome-and-glass elevator, pressed what seemed to be the top button, and turned to face front as the doors closed. He stared forward, looking right through Braintree and, beyond him, the Opuses, as if they weren't even there.

The old man dashed back into the ballroom, ignoring a volley of questions from Jax's bewildered parents. He stuck both forefingers into the sides of his mouth and emitted a piercing whistle that cut right through the raucous aftermath of the press conference. He was good at whistling, a skill he'd learned in prison.

It was the emergency signal. The sandmen knew he'd never use it unless the situation was dire. They came instantly, dropping what they were doing, and more than a few wallets.

Braintree spread his arms, gathering them into a huddle.

There wasn't much time.

Through the spotless glass of the elevator, Jax watched the lobby fall away before him. How beautiful it was, he thought. He wasn't usually the kind of kid who noticed stuff like that. But in his state of euphoria, the whole world was a diorama created just to dazzle him. The chrome accents glittered, and the vast drapery seemed to float rather than hang in the atrium, a colossal golden manta ray standing guard over the Hotel Galaxy. Jax was a part of this majestic ecosystem. The magnificent feeling would last forever if he did his part to keep it thriving. It seemed utterly fair and reasonable. In fact, he considered himself lucky to be included in the wonder. And it was all thanks to Dr. Elias Mako, who had devoted his life to New York City education and was an inspiration to every single one of us.

With a subtle chime, the car reached fourteen, the top floor of the atrium. Jax stepped out onto the mezzanine and peered over the rail to the lobby floor, nearly two hundred feet down. He could hardly wait to experience that distance, to float gracefully down, as if riding a cloud. Dr. Mako had suggested a swan dive, but had left the details entirely up to Jax.

He wasn't much of a diver, but he was pretty sure he could manage to be graceful. He didn't want to spoil something so perfect.

Jax swung a leg over the rail and raised both arms in a diver's pose. This had to be exactly right. He might not ever get another chance. . . .

Not since the night the Berlin Wall came down had so many hypnotists bent so many people in such a short period of time. Axel Braintree and the Sandman's Guild raced around the ballroom, staring into faces and speaking urgently. Within seconds, an army of recruits poured out into the lobby.

In the rush, a few heads turned skyward. Cries of alarm rang out as spectators spied the tiny figure climbing over the rail fourteen stories up. But most of the stampeders were mesmerized. They were utterly focused on the job at hand — nothing more, nothing less.

"This way!" Axel Braintree exploded from the midst of the crowd and led his surging army to the acres of billowing curtains that draped the front windows. Ruthlessly, the mob grasped at the golden hems.

A shriek was torn from Mrs. Opus as she recognized the small form poised to jump from great height.

"No!!!" bellowed her husband in horror.

And then Jackson Opus stepped out into thin air.

He dropped, genuinely astounded that he wasn't floating. His desperate parents tried to rush forward in an illogical attempt to catch him or die trying. Jax spotted them for just a split second. But the next thing he knew, they disappeared, and something big and gold was in the way.

Braintree's sandmen and their brigade of mesmerized civilians backed up across the lobby, stretching the silk curtain panels as taut as they could hold them. Jax fell forty feet, struck the fabric, and began to slide, his progress slowing as the angle of the drapery flattened out. Nearing the bottom, he went into a roll, bowled out three of his rescuers, and hit the floor. It was a hard landing, but not nearly as hard as the one Sentia's director had planned for him.

His trance broken by the impact, he stared up at the circle of faces that surrounded him. "What —?" The last thing he remembered was standing opposite Dr. Mako in the aftermath of the press conference.

The crowd let go of the curtain, which swept like a wave back across the lobby. Through the receding panels burst the curious and the anxious. Most had missed the drama in the atrium, but it was becoming obvious that something had occurred here that was even more tumultuous than Trey Douglas's unexpected withdrawal from the presidential race. In the lead sprinted Mom and Dad, wild with relief. Jax was nearly crushed in their embrace, and he was thrilled to be there. He was thrilled to be anywhere.

The tearful reunion was interrupted by a hammerblow straight to Jax's mind. He looked across the atrium to see Mako in the doorway of the ballroom, glaring at him with naked hatred and malice.

Oh, no, you don't. Not this time!

Jax stared back, totally focused, putting everything he had into repelling this blitz. For a breathless moment, there were only two people in the hotel, locked in a kind of combat that was invisible to the throng around them. On one side, the most experienced hypnotist alive; on the other, the twelve-year-old heir to the legendary bloodlines of Opus and Sparks. A colossal standoff.

Braintree stepped between them, taking the brunt of Mako's assault with his own powerful eyes.

Jax tried to shove him aside. "Get out of the way, man! This isn't your fight!"

The guild president's gaze never wavered from Mako. "It was my fight before you were born."

It took the combined efforts of the New York Police Department and the United States Secret Service to bring the confrontation to a close. They surrounded Senator Douglas and escorted him out of the hotel along with his entourage — which included Mako.

Before Sentia's director joined his one-time candidate and friend, he turned to the Opus party and snarled, "This isn't over."

Jax had a sinking feeling that this was one of the rare times Dr. Mako was telling the truth.

Mr. Opus's strident voice reverberated through the apartment. "What do you mean, 'leave'?"

"You heard Mako, Dad," Jax reasoned. "He's going to come after us again. He can get into our heads! Look at what almost happened today alone. You tried to jump in front of a subway train, and I thought I could fly. If it weren't for Axel . . ."

There was no need to finish that sentence. The Opuses knew perfectly well what would have happened without the president of the Sandman's Guild. Their son would be dead, and they almost certainly would not be around to mourn him.

"We're very grateful to Axel," Mrs. Opus assured her son. "If we neglected to thank him at the hotel, it was only because we were both in shock. And he was pretty angry with his sandmen at the time. Who would have thought hypnotists would turn out to be such crooks?"

Her husband chose that moment to inspect his fingernails. This was no time to bring up the family history he'd worked so hard to forget.

Jax stuck up for the guild members. "Those 'crooks'

came through for us big-time when we needed them. But we can't expect them to stand guard outside our apartment building. When Mako comes back for us, we have to be gone!"

Mr. Opus stubbornly refused to understand. "You mean *move*?"

"Not just move," Jax argued. "We have to change our names and go someplace nobody knows us. Like a kind of witness-protection program for hypnotism."

"We can't do that!" Mom sputtered in outrage. "Your father has a job; I have a practice. It's taken years to build our careers to where we are today! You want us to toss all that in the garbage over your . . . hocus pocus?"

"There's nothing magic about diving off a fourteenth-story balcony," Jax insisted. "Even if science can't explain how Mako made me do it, it still happened. And I'd be dead-dead, not fantasy-dead, if I'd hit the floor. The same goes for jumping in front of trains, or off bridges, or lighting yourself on fire, or anything else you can be convinced to do when you're bent!" He spread his arms wide. "You of all people should listen, Mom. They *named* this stuff after Mesmer, and he was your *cousin*!"

"*Distant* cousin," she said stiffly.

"*Very* distant," her husband added.

Jax turned on his father. "And compared with *your* relatives, guys like Axel and Mako are amateur night. It's not hocus pocus — it's as real as an earthquake. And if we don't get out of the way, we're going to be flattened."

The Opuses were quiet for a long moment. Jax had not yet won them over, but he could sense that his words were beginning to sink in.

Mr. Opus broke the silence at last. "It's no small thing to uproot your entire life."

"I know, Dad. It won't be easy. But the Sandman's Guild has offered to help."

"Oh, that's a good one!" Mom exclaimed. "I've seen their kind of 'help.' They're probably waiting for us to leave so they can ransack our apartment!"

Dad tried to be reasonable. "What about money? We have some savings, sure. But that's for the future. It's your college fund, Jax."

Jax was grave. "No college will accept me if I'm dead."

His parents just stared at him.

Jax came back to himself with a shiver to see Axel Braintree smiling reassuringly at him. He stretched, almost knocking over the folded chiropractor's table that was leaning against a stack of boxes in the U-Haul.

"Well?" he asked nervously.

In less than twenty-four hours, the Opuses had upended their lives, packed what they could, and were about to leave New York forever. All that would be for nothing if Sentia's director had implanted any strategic suggestions inside Jax's mind. Mako was a compulsive schemer to the point of genius, and Jax had just spent more than two months under the man's thumb. Would the director be able to hurt him somehow, or compel him to hurt himself, even from a distance? Or perhaps Jax harbored some sort of mesmeric architecture that would serve as a tracking device. That would be just as dangerous. Very little was beyond the capability of a hypnotist like Mako.

There was no way for Jax to inspect himself for such time bombs, so he had allowed himself to be bent and examined by the president of the Sandman's Guild.

"It's quite a nifty piece of mind-tinkering," Braintree admitted grudgingly. "You carry a suggestion to forget everything you know about Mako and Sentia."

"I knew it," Jax growled. "I've heard stories about ex-hypnos who don't even recognize the people they worked with every day. What's the trigger?"

"That's the genius of it," the old man told him. "There isn't one."

"But I remember every hole in every ceiling tile of that place," Jax protested. "I wish I didn't, but I do."

"There's a separate suggestion, postponing the command to forget. And the trigger for *that* is neither a word nor an action."

Jax frowned. "Then what is it?"

"A face. She's a real looker, too. Blonde, blue-eyed. In my day, they called a woman like that 'a dish.'"

Jax nodded. "Maureen Samuels, the assistant director. She's the first person you see when you arrive, and the last when you go home."

The old man's brow furrowed. "You haven't been there in more than a week. That should have been more than enough time to wipe your mind clean."

Shamefaced, Jax produced his cell phone and switched it on. The lock screen showed a picture of himself standing next to the beautiful Ms. Samuels. "It was just to show the guys at school," he confessed. "I guess I never got around to deleting it."

Braintree chuckled. "Even the Great Mako can't think of everything. He should have hired Quasimodo, not Marilyn Monroe. Anyway, you don't have to worry about it. I disabled both suggestions."

Jax gave him a rueful smile. "For a guy who formed a whole guild to convince sandmen not to use hypnotism, you're pretty smooth at it."

The old man shrugged. "It's a gift. That's the whole problem. One minute you're saving the world; the next, you're down at the bank, bending the manager to give you a tour of the vault."

Mrs. Opus heaved two suitcases over the tailgate. "That's the last of it. Your father's gone to take the Bentley back to the dealership. He keeps tearing up, so don't talk about it."

"Believe me, I won't," Jax promised soberly. "You think I feel good about this? I can't even believe it's happening."

She sighed but put on a brave face. "We'll leave as soon as he gets back."

"That gives me a little more time," Jax acknowledged. "There's one last thing I have to take care of."

33

The corridors of I.S. 222 looked strange to Jax, mostly because he knew he would probably never lay eyes on them again. Funny — there had been days when he would have given anything to get away from this dumpy old building with its smell of sweat socks and stale pizza. Now he was nostalgic about the place, like it was home sweet home.

Maybe it was this: He hadn't really had time to mourn the disaster that had come over his family. Mom and Dad, ripped from their lives and careers, thanks to him. And all of them abandoning New York, the only hometown he'd ever known or ever wanted to know. Easier to say good-bye to a rusty row of lockers than to admit that the Jackson Opus he'd been for twelve years no longer existed. In a couple of days, he'd be somebody else from somewhere else, and that was unthinkable.

It was the middle of eighth period and the halls were empty. That was a good thing. He didn't feel like explaining over and over again what had happened since he'd fallen down the stairs and knocked himself silly. Not that anyone would have believed his story. He barely believed it himself.

Eighth period — French. He pressed his body against the door and peered in through the small window until he'd caught Tommy's eye. Tommy was up like a shot and out to join him.

"I thought you were dead, Opus! I texted you, like, six hundred times!"

Jax hauled his friend into the nearest bathroom. "We have to talk."

"Tell me about it! Did you hear the news about your man Trey Douglas? CNN called it the biggest political meltdown since Watergate!"

"Bigger," said Jax. "In Watergate, President Nixon was bent face-to-face by a staffer. I got Trey Douglas through his teleprompter."

"You're not making any sense, man! What's going on?"

Instead of answering, Jax looked deep into his friend's eyes.

Tommy was insulted. "You're trying to *hypnotize* me? What for?"

"Relax . . ." Jax intoned. "You are becoming very calm. . . ."

"No, I'm not," Tommy spat back. "I'm becoming very ticked off! What's with you, Opus? You know you can't hypnotize me!"

Jax ramped up the intensity of his stare. It was true. He'd never been able to bend Tommy Cicerelli. He also understood he had to find a way to make it work this time, for his friend's sake. It was one thing for Jax's own family to suffer, but Tommy was an innocent bystander.

Mako had already found Tommy, had mesmerized him at least once. The boy would never be safe as long as he knew about Sentia and the Trey Douglas affair.

Jax had told him too much already.

"Fine," Tommy snapped. "Bring it on, Merlin. Do your worst. I'm color-blind, remember? I've got you beat! To me, your famous eyes are gray on gray!"

That makes it hard, not impossible, Jax thought, sharpening his focus. *I fought off Elias Mako last night! I'm an Opus and a Sparks, and I can do this!*

When the PIP image appeared between them, Jax realized instantly that it could only be coming from Tommy. He saw himself in black-and-white, and the dark green bathroom stalls were a smoky charcoal.

Jax wasted no time. Already this intrusion into his friend's mind stung like a terrible betrayal. If he hung around much longer, Tommy's thoughts and feelings would begin to leach into his own, and life was tough enough already today.

"When you wake up, you'll feel relaxed and happy. And this is very important: You will remember nothing of Jackson Opus's ability to perform hypnotism. You will forget everything he ever told you about the Sentia Institute and the Sandman's Guild. You will have no recollection of . . ."

He recited a laundry list of every possible detail Tommy might have picked up over Jax's weeks at Sentia. Never in his brief career as a hypnotist had he been so thorough and so precise. If he left Tommy with one single memory that might somehow land the kid on Mako's radar screen, disaster would surely follow. Jax had turned his own family inside out. If he allowed Tommy to suffer, he'd never forgive himself.

When he finished, he found himself panting as if he'd just won a marathon. There remained one more thing for him to say, and it was the most painful of all.

"Anyway, you and Jackson Opus were never that close," he murmured, choking up just a little. "You barely know the guy, so it doesn't really bother you that he's not around anymore."

He left his friend, his school, his life. He barely noticed the bustling city around him as he retraced his path to the loaded U-Haul.

It was time to disappear off the face of the earth.